PUBLISHING
L.L.C.

Books by Annalisa Conti:

Nine, a novel (2018)
Africa, a novel (2015)
All The People, a novel (2014)

W Is For Wonder, a collection of short stories (2018)

The W Series, short stories (from 2016)

W IS FOR WONDER

ANNALISA CONTI

Published by AEC Publishing LLC in New York

www.annalisaconti.com

ISBN-13: 978-1-7321992-8-6
ISBN-10: 1-7321992-8-0

W IS FOR WONDER,
a collection of short stories

To Emmanuel

CONTENTS

ANNALISA CONTI

WRONG DAY FOR A KILL

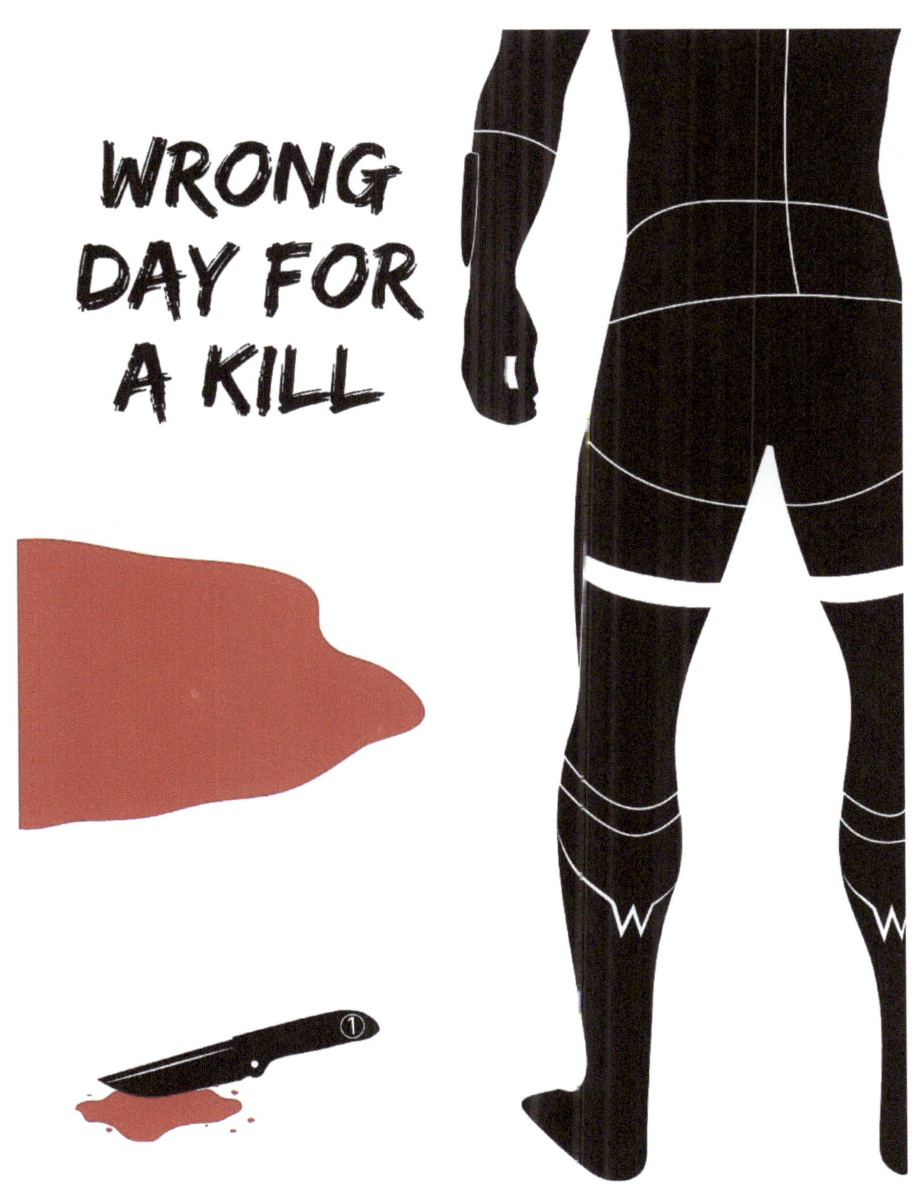

Annalisa Conti

WRONG DAY FOR A KILL

Run.

Keep running, ass-holes. I can run faster than you, you know it, and I'll get you in the end.

"Hey! Ass-holes! I said stop!"

They never listen, ever. But I like yelling at them, I like the way my voice sounds when I'm wearing the mask: it's so loud, so scary. I can feel they fear me. Jay did a great job with this new voice modulator: the sound is really smooth and the tone is just perfect. He also added some lower frequencies that mess up with people's neuronal connections, they make them subconsciously shiver. It's great. And the mask now goes well with the suit, total black: it hides me and lets me blend in with the night, in the dark corners of this city.

"Ouch!"

What the hell was that? Did he just throw a bag of garbage at me? You jerk, you'll learn how to behave with W! I know, the name is not very evocative, but it's right for me: W for wonder, W for watchman, W for… well, W for a lot of other things. I'm sick of you, man, I've been following you and your buddy in this labyrinth of dark alleys for too long: I'm glad I got there in time to save that poor girl from your disgusting claws, you junkies, but our little chase is rather annoying. I don't even know if you just wanted to rob her, to buy more stuff to clog your veins with, or if you also wanted to rape her, for a nice all-included night full of fun. I despise you, anyway, sometimes I despise all East Harlem and its jungle of darkness and lost souls.

"I said stop!"

He must be deaf, or just too stupid to understand who he's facing - better, who is running after him. And where is his buddy now? He must have gone hiding somewhere, looking for some fast consolation in a last sip of cheap alcohol, or at the bottom of a syringe. This is taking too long now, let me show you how bad your night is going to become.

It's easy to get guys like him, in the end: I just need to speed up a little bit, keep yelling at him to scare him out, wait for him to turn his head back towards me, to check how close I am, and stumble, slow down. That's usually where I get them, and this one is not different.

I hold him by his neck, glad to have gloves and not to have to touch his filthy clothes or his grayish skin. I hold him high up against the wall of the old building, in another abandoned dark street; his eyes are right in front of mine: my eyes are covered by the mask and he can't see them, but I can see the fear and the astonishment in his dilated pupils.

"Where do you think you're going?"

"What the fuck do you care? Who the hell are you? You're not the Police."

"See, you're not that stupid: I'm not the Police. I'm worse!"

I hold him slightly tighter and his eyes open up more, his eyebrows climb up higher, giving to his whole face a grotesque look. He doesn't move, his dark hair flows in a gust of cold wind that rolls up from the East River and gets channeled all the way down here. It smells like sadness.

"If you're not the Police then let go of me, what do you think you are? You're crazy!"

He tries to kick me in the balls, but I come closer and block his legs with mine, while I close my hand even tighter around his neck. He starts suffocating, and he tries to hit my arm with a punch, but I'm faster than him and I block that, as well: now he's completely stuck.

"Now that we can talk," I love how bold I can sound sometimes, "Let me explain the situation to you: I'm going to tie you up like Italian salami and kick you in the ass until we reach the closest Police Station. What do you think? Do you like the idea? I'm sure you're close friends with the Detectives down there."

And it will make me so happy to piss off the Commissioner once again, so that maybe he'll finally stop saying that he doesn't need me, and that I'm a crazy weirdo.

With one hand I take a couple of plastic handcuffs out of a pocket in my suit, spending a fraction of a second being amazed by how Jay could fit pockets, and stuff in them, in this suit. But let's be honest: this suit is not that tight, there's plenty of room on the inside, plenty of composite foam that both protects me and enhances my shape. I love these carbon-fiber-made muscles! With a swift move I tie the junkie's ankles, so that his legs don't bother me anymore, and then I'm ready to handcuff his wrists. He makes a grimace when I look at him again in the eyes, close enough to smell his foul breath.

"What now? Feel like laughing?"

Something changes in his eyes, what the h…

"Argh!" I cry out loud.

What's this damned pain in my back? Argh! I can't control my arms anymore, I have to let the junkie fall; something hit me between my shoulders! What's going on? The jerk is laughing hard now, pointing at something behind me. His buddy has just reached us and he's holding a knife in his hand; the knife is dripping blood from its long blade. My blood. The ass-hole stabbed me between my shoulders. My back is burning, I can't breathe, I think I'll fall. I look at the man who just stabbed me, and I my eyes turn foggy: pain, rage. Rage.

I completely forget junkie number one to channel all my remaining strength towards junkie number two: he just tried to kill me! Something takes hold of me: blood flows in my veins, stronger, faster, it keeps coming out from the long wound in my back, but it also keeps running up to my brain. I'm a bull in the bullfight arena: I've been hit and my eyes are red with blood and rage. Rage. Adrenaline. My body doesn't respond to my will, instead it reacts to answer to some animal instinct of survival. I jump up and grab junkie number two's head with my left hand, I seize his face in my palm and look at his eyes, now wide open in terror: he just realized he has made a mistake. I'm stronger than him, even with my back torn apart; I'm taller, faster. He's hopeless. I'm still holding his skull in my hand, and with all my strength I crash it against the wall in front of me.

In this very second a few things happen: junkie number one screams and runs away, after having somehow untied his ankles; all adrenaline and excitement flow off my brain; junkie number two's head cracks open, blood spills out and splashes all over the place, on the wall and on my suit, on my mask, on my left glove that's still holding his head.

I suddenly let him go, and he collapses down on the ground. He doesn't move.

"Fuck."

I can't say anything else, I can't think anything else. Did I kill him? Did I just kill a man? I had never killed a man before: I had been in a lot of fights, shootings, shit, but never killed a man. What the hell happened to me?

"You cannot die, ass-hole."

I can't be responsible of your death. I'm here to protect this city, not to kill its people, not even the lowest forms of life, like you, jerk. You cannot die.

I tear off a piece of his jacket and I wrap his head in it to try to stop the bleeding, but there's a lot of blood and I know I have to call an ambulance. I know nothing about reanimation techniques, I'm completely useless here.

What have I done?

I can smell the stink of panic starting to creep up my back, climbing up my spine; it tickles the back of my head, where my neck ends and my skull starts; it whispers rambling words of fear in my ears; it covers my eyes with its greedy hands. But I can't freeze now, I can't panic: I have to try to save this man, even if he doesn't deserve it, even if he's just a junkie, even if he tried to rob and maybe rape a girl to get some more drugs. I can't panic.

How do I call an ambulance? I don't have a phone in this suit: Jay put countless tech crap in it, but not a phone or an IP connection device of any sort. Damn it, Jay, you should be the smart one here! How do I call an ambulance?

How do I call a fucking ambulance?

Think Guinn, think. No phone, maybe a pay phone? Yeah, right, we're in New York, I can't even remember when I've seen the last pay phone in the street. Think Guinn, think! I need to look for a phone, maybe I can go in a Duane Reade or something and ask for the phone? Yeah right, dressed like the poor cousin of Batman, with this stupid suit and all. Ok, I'll remove the suit, maybe freezing my ass in this February wind will give me some ideas. God, it's really cold without the suit, but at least I'm wearing a t-shirt and pants, and I'm not just in my underwear like I was doing until December:

this suit is so hot. Jay used the best isolating and protective composite materials that he could get his hands on, a lot of off-the-record top-secret stuff he sort of borrowed at work: he's the best Materials Engineer I've ever met. God, it's freaking cold without the suit! I can't think with this cold!

Think Guinn, think! I hide my suit behind a trash can and I start to walk back to the street where the two junkies were attacking the girl, hoping for some ideas to reach my dumb mind, for some inspiration to get to me, somehow. Time flies here: every second I waste lowers the chances the guy has to survive. I can't be responsible for his death, not me, not today: it's not a good day for killing a man. What do I do now? I want to scream.

"Fuck!"

There's nobody around, and why should anybody want to walk around at this time, with this cold, in this shitty area? At least nobody sees me walking around bare feet in these tight pants. Crap, there's nothing open here, what the hell do I do now? The guy will die, the damned guy will die and it will be my fault. What kind of a monster have I become? I struggle to kick the panic back again: I have to think fast, faster, or the guy will die and it will be my fault.

Wait, there's somebody down there. He just passed the corner. A guy. He's walking a few feet in front of me. Can I ask him his phone to call 911? He will never let me use it: he will think I'm a crazy person, he will start screaming and he will run away. Should I steal his phone? I can knock him out with one blow, a very light touch on the back of his neck: he won't even realize that anything happened. And I can take his phone and call the ambulance.

It only takes a second: run, strike, dial.

"911?"

"I need an ambulance at the corner of Third Avenue and 123rd street: a man is bleeding out from his head."

"The ambulance is on its way; please spell your first name and last n…"

The hell. I hang up and wake up the guy, but I disappear before he can see me and eventually recognize me. I run back to junkie number two: the situation is bad here. He's still alive but now I'm even more convinced that he will die, and it will be my fault. What have I done? There's so much blood in here. What do I do?

The ambulance arrives really fast and I run hiding in the dark: I put my suit back on and they can't see me hidden above them, on a fire escape. I kneel, I pray the guy can survive, I pray I haven't killed him. I've never killed anyone, I'm not a killer, I'm a good person. I'm the good guy here, this damned junkie is the bad guy in this story, so why do I have to feel so shitty if he dies? Probably just because I'm the good guy: good guys never really win, we always feel guilty because we didn't completely defeat the bad guys, or we didn't do enough, or we didn't teach a good enough lesson, or we didn't save everybody, or just because we're human beings and we can't save this whole shitty world. Damn it.

"We have a man bleeding from the head, skull fracture, brain matter exposed," ambulance guy number one is talking to the radio, while ambulance guy number two and three warily take junkie number two's vital signs trying not to move him.

"He looks like he's been bleeding for several minutes: he already lost a lot of blood. Give me two units of O negative, and let's try to wrap his head up, before we lose his brains."

Ambulance guy number two looks like the boss: ambulance guy number one and three are promptly following his orders. They have attached the junkie to a portable heart monitor, which suddenly launches a long high beep.

"We're losing him! Give me one milligram of epinephrine, take the defibrillator, and let's start the heart massage."

"One, two, three, four, five… One, two, three, four, five… Defibrillator, now!"

"Hands off!"

"Confirmed VT and VF."

"Stand clear charging! Charge 200! Stand clear shocking!"

The junkie shakes all up while they're administering the shock, but the beep is still continuous. Things don't look good. The ambulance guys get ready to try again.

"Stand clear charging! Charge 360, stand clear shocking!"

They keep charging and delivering. Come on junkie, be a man and try to survive. Time runs, I can feel the seconds ticking in my brains, my breaths become shorter and more anguishing, while the ambulance people keep pushing and charging and electrocuting the junkie.

Everything is suddenly quiet.

"Time of death: 3:18 am."

Now I'm a killer, I'm an actual killer. Now in what am I different from the bad guys? I killed a man. I didn't want to, but I killed a man. Everything suddenly shuts down: I can't hear the noises of the ambulance people anymore, I can't here the siren anymore, or the wind blowing in the alley. I can't hear my own heart beating in my chest anymore: is it still there? Maybe I'm dead, too, just like the junkie. Suddenly a sharp sting in my back: I had forgotten about it, but the wound is still bleeding; I twist my arm to try and touch my shoulder blade but it's too painful, I can only brush against the large sprain in my suit. I'm still kneeling in the fire escape, I bend my back to rest my head on my thighs and I let my hands grab my cranium. I close my eyes. What have I done? What have I become?

I killed a man.

I open my eyes again and I suddenly realize it's raining a sharp frozen rain: it's too cold even to be snowing. I stretch my back and look up to the sky, I look at the frozen drops falling on my mask; the traces they leave make my sight blurry, the pain in my back makes it foggy. I should go home.

I softly walk down the fire escape stairs, then down and up and left and right on the streets, hiding from the light of the pale lamps, hiding from my own thoughts.

I killed a man.

I walk. I keep my shoulders low while I get lost in my own city, not even looking around to see where I'm headed; I roam in the darkness for what look like hours, covered in a corrosive rain, thanking Jay for the waterproof coating on the suit. I feel and look like a black worm crawling out of its hole in the ground, a black killer maggot, a despicable thing that anybody with a soul would want to squash under their shoe.

I killed a man.

Somehow I get to the building that I call home, while a grey light starts to illuminate the sky from behind heavy clouds: it's already morning. I slowly climb up the fire escape and slither through the open window, in the darkness of an empty room. Almost empty.

"Where the hell have you been?! I thought you were dead!"

Jay turns on the bedside light: his eyes remain in the shadows, but the pale yellow luminescence gives his face evil features.

"I asked you where the hell have you been!"

I don't want to speak. I remove my mask and my suit's hood, keeping my gaze low and letting my hair fall on my forehead and cover my eyes. I finally look at him; he stares at my face and he realizes right away that something is wrong. He comes closer and helps me remove the suit.

He sees the deep cut in the back of the suit, in my t-shirt and in my skin. He knows it will be gone in a few hours, but he realizes it hurts, and he looks at me right in the eyes, "What happened?"

"I killed a man."

I know him: he's scared. He doesn't look at me in the eyes anymore.

"Did he do this to you?"

"Yes."

"Then you were just defending yourself."

I'm out of my suit, sitting on the bed in my room. He goes to his bedroom to grab his first aid kit: he knows the wound will be completely healed in a few hours without even leaving a scar, he knows that I don't get infections, that I haven't been sick since I've gotten my powers, that I am stronger than any other human being, but he still wants to disinfect my skin. Just because. I let him do it: it makes him feel better, it gives him time to think. It tickles.

"How do you feel?"

"I feel like somebody who just killed a man."

"Stop it right away: you're not a murderer, you were just defending yourself."

"It doesn't matter."

He lowers his head and his eyes fall on the suit that now lies balled up on the bed, thick layers of composite materials. He takes it in his hands and he calmly stretches it out on the bed: he looks at the long black legs, the torso and the arms with the sculpted muscles, to enhance the look and feel of my skinny upper body; he puts the mask above the hood, he aligns the black boots with the side of the bed. Then he looks at me and he seems to remember how thin and fragile I look when I am not wearing the suit.

"Don't let my body fool you: you know how strong I am, you know I'm much stronger than he was and I knew it, too. I knew it but I couldn't control myself. I couldn't control my rage: when he stabbed me, I let my fear take control of me, and now he's dead. I'll never forget his face, his viscid junkie face."

"Stop condemning yourself, it was not your fault!"

"It was: what kind of a protector can I be for this city if I can't even protect its weakest members, the people who suffer and find themselves in trouble, like that junkie? I don't have the right to take a life."

"You had to save yourself, and sometimes hard decisions need to be made for a greater good."

I don't agree, and he knows it. He has been saying this since the first time he discovered my powers, he keeps talking about it: the greater good, whatever the hell it is. He talks about justice, but I don't even know what this means here and now. Does killing a bad guy produce more justice? Can killing somebody be rationalized as a component of the bigger scheme of things, in which the only part that matters is the result, the ultimate goal of enforcing justice?

"If this is the price to pay, if killing people is the price to pay, then this is not worth it. This was a mistake."

"You are the only one who can help this city, you are the only one who can bring justice to this God-forsaken place."

Justice, this nonsense word again.

"You talk about justice, but who are we to define what justice is? We're not in College anymore, where you speak words just to impress the professors or the girl sitting next to you. This is the real life, Jay, and we're nobody: we're just two idiots who thought they could save the world."

"We're not idiots: I know you can save the world, this world, from itself, from its corruption and its flaws. You're the person for the job."

"I'm not the guy for the job, I'm just a guy in a black suit."

"A suit that is a symbol of everything that you can be!"

"A suit that makes me appear taller and bigger, with a mask that makes my voice sound scary. I'm not a symbol, I'm a scam!"

"You're not a scam, you have powers! Remember: W is for wonderful, W is for watcher."

"W is for weak."

His eyes brighten up and he almost smiles, "W is for woman, this is why you're the person for the job, this is why you're better than any other guy who ever tried to save this city from itself!"

All of a sudden I seem to remember: W is for woman, this is what I am. A woman, a stupid girl who thinks she can save the world. Well, I clearly can't.

He must be thinking something completely different, because he keeps smiling. I don't.

"Remember Guinn, W is for wish, W is for hope: you're the only hope to build a better New York, a better world."

His words plug up my throat, they stop the air from flowing in and out for a few seconds. I don't cry because I'm not good at crying, but I feel sorry for this city: it threw itself into a black pit of suffering and desperation, and now there's nothing left to do. I feel sorry for him, too, especially for him: Jay is my best friend, he has been since our years in college, a long time ago, but when he discovered my powers he saw something else in me. Suddenly I was not his buddy Guinn anymore, I was not the girl he used to study and get drunk with after each test. Suddenly I was hope, I was a possible solution, a cause to dedicate himself to. He sees in me much more than I've ever seen in myself, than I ever will. It breaks my heart to disappoint him.

I just look at him, "Then I'm sorry, but hope died tonight: I smashed its head against a wall."

WOMAN
IN BLACK
Annalisa Conti

WOMAN IN BLACK

"You look really terrible," the words gently slide out of Shaila's mouth between two sips of chai latte.

I almost spit my green tea out of my nose: no shit. I killed a man just three months ago, almost to the day, in a frozen February night, and now the sweeter winds of spring are still barely warm enough to keep me alive. The first weeks after the fact were possessed by a tangled laziness, as I kept my brain switched off not to think about that night, about those eyes drowning in terror while I was smashing the back of his skull against the wall. For weeks Jay had to be my therapist, a very special one who treats his only patient with beers instead of medications, during long nightly sessions. When I lie on our sofa, after unspecified numbers of six-packs have been emptied, I can swear I see an aura of light surrounding him, making him look like the Indian guru he probably was in another life, my friend Jayashandra. Then I usually pass out. Somehow he still manages to wake up before dawn every day, to go to his job in New Jersey. The first time he told me he had been hired by the Army to work in a top-secret underground lab in the abandoned base of Fort Monmouth, to develop innovative defense materials, he looked like he had won the lottery. Then he realized it would take him almost two hours to reach his work place, and he got suddenly less excited.

"Thank you for you kind words," I grin back to Shaila. "You know how to make somebody feel better."

"So I'm right. What's up?"

"You know, it's just winter's toll: February has always been my least favorite month of the year, and then it takes me a couple more months to recover from it."

"Bullshit," she intertwines the word with a fake cough, to pretend she is not saying it. She is a drama queen in her own way. "I've been living in Spanish Harlem too long not to detect if somebody got something to hide. They already tried to rape me once: fool me twice, shame on me."

Her eyes pierce through mine, they tickle the back of my neck as they dig deeper into my soul, gazing into my past and future like a witch's eyes. A thread has been wrapping us together since the day I first met her, years ago, and later decided to join her yoga class. In the end my two only friends are an Indian guru and a Jamaican witch: way to go, Guinn!

"Anyway babe, whatever your problem, Shaila Peters here has a solution: get laid."

I do my surprised emoji face: never fails to pull a raspy laugh out of her throat.

"I gather you're up for it?"

"Do you have a lucky gentleman in mind, or is it just a general advice?" I can easily pick up guys in bars, but a recommendation is always welcome. Not for a relationship though: how could I explain the nights away, the bruises, the stab wounds, the gun wounds, the black full-body armor made of Kevlar fibers imbided in a matrix of ultra-high-molecular-weight polyethylene glycol, epoxy resin and titanium particles? Too complicated.

"I do actually have somebody in mind, and I would hit on him myself if I was not married," Shaila's eyes start to throw sparkles at me. "He is a new personal trainer at the gym, smoking hot, tall because you need them like seven feet, also seems not too dumb and not a complete douche."

"Yum."

"That's what I thought. I told him you're free on Friday night."

"This Friday? You mean tomorrow?"

"What's wrong? Need more time to shave your legs?" she is classy like that.

"Nope, legs are fine. Let me check my calendar," I look at my phone, as if I had anything planned besides getting drunk on my sofa with Jay. "Free as a bird tomorrow night."

"I figured," Shaila doesn't look surprised. "I already gave him your number. I told him to text you tomorrow morning to make plans."

"Woah, ok. Do you have a picture of the man, at least?"

"Trust me, and thank me on Saturday morning."

The phone vibrates on my desk while I'm speaking with my boss, Tony Sepulveda, on a slow Friday morning in the office.

"I want to land in Brussels on Wednesday morning, since the dinner is that night. Do you think you can find me a flight?" as the President of the global advertising company he founded a few decades ago, and that is now entirely managed by his son, all he does nowadays is travelling around the world to have luxury dinners with his top clients. This leaves me a lot of free time when he's not in the office: the perfect assistant job for somebody with sleepless nights.

I type keywords on my computer, "United has a 6:15 pm that brings you there at 7:40 am, Delta has a 7:35 pm to 9:15 am: which company do you want miles from?"

Agreed on Delta, he leaves the booking process to me. A few minutes and I grab my mobile phone: text from an unknown number.

"Hi this is Matt, I'm Shaila's colleague. How about drinks tonight?"

"Hi, this is Guinn, I'm Shaila's friend. Where do you want to meet?" I think I'm being funny, but sometimes I doubt it myself.

"Nice to meet you – smiley face – 7 pm at Sweet Revenge, 62 Carmine Street?"

"Sounds good. Will you be waiting for me with a rose on the table? – LOL face"

"Shaila showed me your picture, I will recognize you."

Creepy, but fine.

I look at my reflection in the mirror, before leaving my apartment for the night: I see a skinny girl in a short black dress and a ponytail, what will Matt see?

Sweet Revenge is a little bar in Greenwich Village, and I spot Matt as soon as I get in. I'm sure he's the guy sitting alone at a table, with a beer in front of him. Shaila was damn right: very hunky. Before he sees me, I swiftly free my hair from the elastic band and I pass my fingers through it, to give it some shape.

A second later he's smiling back at me: I guess I don't look that different from the picture Shaila showed him. That's a good start.

"Matt?"

"Guinn McGovern?"

"Yes Sir!" I even add the military gesture. Sometimes I'm just an idiot. But he laughs, so maybe Shaila did tell him that I'm a weirdo.

"I'm sorry, that sounded totally stupid. Nice to meet you Guinn," he throws me his hand and I take it in mine, while I sit at the table.

The waiter is standing next to me and I can order a Stella, and pray for it to come quickly. If there's one thing I hate about first dates is those first five minutes, when you are trying to read the other person to decide the first topic of conversation. Some people are fine with a "so how was your day?", while others prefer to be straightforward and might go for a "what's your favorite role in a three-some?". You never know.

"Shaila told me you've been friends for a few years: did you meet her at her yoga class?" he picks a standard opening, no three-some quite yet.

"Right. And did you just start working at the gym?"

"Yes, just a few weeks ago. I moved here from Ohio years ago, but life is getting more and more expensive in New York, so I took the personal trainer job at the gym. Where are you from?"

"San Francisco. I moved here a few years ago, after college. Ah, cheers," I add, a Stella finally in my hand. I force myself not to drink it all in one sip, as I've been doing almost every night for many weeks with Jay. I don't want Matt to think I'm a drunk.

"Cheers," he smiles again at me, a sweet smile on a manly jawbone, hanging on top of a muscular yet sleek body. I think this night is going to be interesting.

"So why did you come to New York City, Guinn from San Francisco?"

"I guess the same reason everybody comes here: for work. When I was in my last year at College I interviewed at a bunch of companies and consulting firms, and I picked a consultancy here in Manhattan."

"Do you still work there? I heard consulting is very tiring," he smiles while he orders a second round of beers for both of us: we have at least one thing in common, we are fast drinkers.

"That's right, and that's exactly why I don't work there anymore: too much work. I have a job in an advertising company now."

"Cool. Did you study marketing in college?"

"No," I realize the tricky part is quickly coming up. "I have a Masters in Engineering from Stanford."

His eyes widen up as most people's when they hear the words Engineering and Stanford in the same sentence.

"Stanford? Where did you say you work?"

"A small advertising company: after years in consulting I was sick of it and I just wanted something quieter," here I have to drop the bomb, for him to stop asking too many questions. "Also, my grandma lives in Brooklyn and she's very sick, so I need to take care of her."

I know I'm a terrible person, but what can I do? My grandma is thankfully a very healthy and witty old Vietnamese lady. She does indeed live in Brooklyn and I see her once in a while. But I need a good excuse to explain why somebody like me ended up working as an old guy's assistant at thirty-four years old, after grad school and almost seven years spent in the top business consulting firm.

The second round of beers quickly sooths my thirst and placates my thoughts. What life would I have if I didn't have my powers, if this curse hadn't found me?

We drink and we talk and I start feeling way more than tipsy. I used to be able to drink more than Jay when we were in college, and many times I had to drag him out of a bar and back to his dorm in the middle of the night, but something happened to me when I got my powers. I mean, something clearly happened to me when I got my powers, but in addition to that I also started to show signs of a sort of allergy to alcohol: now very small quantities make my brain numb. It's like being on drugs. It all goes away in less than one hour, according to Jay's scientific observations, but man, how long an hour can be!

"Do you mind if we get something to eat?" I hear myself asking. Such a shame: two beers, maybe three, and I need something solid in my stomach! "Or do you want to go somewhere else for dinner?"

"I would love to have a real dinner, but I can't."

What?

"I know, it sucks, but I have to go to work in about one hour, maybe one and a half," he mumbles with vivid regret in his eyes.

"You have to go do your personal training on Friday night at like ten? Isn't it a bit late?" I usually smell lies from afar, but strangely enough this doesn't even sound like one.

"It is, I mean it would. I thought Shaila told you: I work at the gym only a few nights per week and sometimes on weekends; in my daylight life I'm a research assistant, and I have the shittiest shifts this week."

He gets from the curious look on my face that no, I didn't know it.

"What type of research do you do?" I have two conflicting thoughts in my mind regarding my next step tonight: since he has little more than one hour to spend with me, we could just go to my place, or his, and get decently laid, because that's the reason I came out tonight. And I shaved my legs. But he suddenly sounds more intriguing than I thought, and I might want to talk to him a bit longer. I will give him ten more minutes, and then I will call an Uber.

"Medical research. I work with vaccines."

"It sounds so cool!" I shouldn't have drunk the third beer: I would have had a more intelligent commentary.

"Thank you," he blushes lightly. "It is very important research: we are developing some innovative types of vaccines, built on a combination of gene-based therapy and antibodies. Am I boring you already?"

I gesture to please keep talking.

"Awesome! I work with Professor Hoffmann, I don't know if you heard about him," I shake my head. "He is one of the world experts in multi-clonal antibody therapy, who has been dedicating the last fifteen years of his career to constructing a completely new concept of vaccines. His idea is that personalized vaccines could be developed, to train the body of each specific individual to respond to any type of disease. This has a million potential indications, from vaccinations against cancer to faster healing of wounds, regeneration of brain cells, increased muscular tone and strength, potentially anything!"

I can hear my heart missing a beat in my chest, and then suddenly accelerating until I think it's going to make a hole in my torso and run away.

"Are you ok, Guinn?" he notices.

"Yes, I am. Sorry, I drank too much too fast. You were saying?"

"I was saying: anything could be possible. Professor Hoffmann is one of the most talented brains I have met in my life, and he is completely devoted to his research. A few years ago there was an accident in the research facility: I wasn't working there at the time, so I've only heard some rumors about the fire, but he lost everything. All his documents and his records, all his samples, everything. He didn't lose his faith in himself and his work, though: he rebuilt a brand new facility on the ashes of the old one, in the same lot in the Lower East Side; he didn't hesitate to restart from scratch, because this is the most important thing in his life."

His eyes are almost watering, as are mine, but for completely different reasons.

"The accident happened a few years ago, you said?" I can barely breathe.

"Let me think about it… I think it was ten years ago, maybe nine. Nine."

I need to throw up.

"Can you excuse me for a second? I need to use the ladies' room."

I do my best not to rush to the bathroom, but when I'm in I lock myself in the first free stall and I throw up everything I have in me. With an empty stomach, but still hugging the toilet bowl, my thoughts start to align in front of my eyes: the facility burned down nine years ago, in the Lower East Side. Nine years ago I woke up after a night out in the Lower East Side with some inhuman powers that interestingly resemble the medical characteristics of Matt's vaccines: a knife wound heals in a couple of hours, I am stronger than any other human being, my brain works faster – is it because of enhanced cell regeneration? Jay and I had never thought about this, and I'm astonished by how much sense it makes.

I hadn't wondered about the origins of my powers in a long time: I got used to them, I guess, and I learned to live with them, rather than fight them or keep asking myself why me? The why-me phase lasted for years, at the very beginning: I've always believed in causality, action and reaction, Newton's laws of motion, and those powers clearly didn't fit with any of it. I hadn't done anything wrong in my life: I had studied and worked hard, I had respected people and treated them right, I had visited my grandparents every weekend. I had always been a good person, and now I found myself completely screwed, like the time I broke Jay's ribs because I couldn't control my strength. I'm a monster for no reason.

In the bathroom I try to wash away the vomit-green hue from my face. I don't know what time is it, but I need to go back outside and learn from Matt as much as I can. Can there really be a connection?

"Sorry I kept you waiting," I nonchalantly pull out a chewing gum from my purse, as I get closer to him in the suddenly more crowded and louder bar. "Your story is so interesting! Do you know if the professor had any results before the accident? If any tests were conducted on humans?"

"I don't think so: the research is still preliminary now, and I assume we are far beyond where he was nine years ago. I think at the time he just had a lot of theoretical research and machines that hadn't been fully installed; he had some work-in-progress samples of modified antibodies, but nothing would have actually worked at the time."

I can't stop my brain to run on its own path: something doesn't fit here, because I am the result of much more than a work in progress. Something did work, even too well. Maybe Matt is still fairly new and he doesn't know all the details, or maybe he and the Professor are hiding something.

"When did you move to New York, you said?" I test my interrogation skills, learned from watching at least five seasons of C.S.I. and countless detective movies.

"A few years ago."

"And have you been working in the research facility with Professor Hoffmann since then?"

"I have," an interrogative look shows up on his face.

"Sorry was it weird?" I laugh, covering my eyes with my hands, and I act girly: this always distracts them. "I think I'm a bit drunk, I'm usually not that inquisitive!"

A few years can be a long time. Does Matt know more than what he's saying? Can I trust him? I guess there's only one way to know it.

The drunken girl card always works: he relaxes and he smiles back at me, "No worries, I guess it's my fault: we kept drinking without feeding you."

"How much time do you have?"

He fishes in his pocket looking for his cell phone, "I have to be at work in about one hour: I need to move two samples from the centrifuge to the analyzer."

"So you have to be in the Lower East Side in about one hour, right?"

He nods.

"Where do you live?" I figure I'd ask, before ordering the Uber.

His facial expression is hard to interpret: some incredulity, some excitement, "Murray Hill," The bar is now so loud that he has to speak right in my ear. I take advantage of the proximity to caress his face and kiss him, hoping I don't stink of vomit. He kisses me back with his taste of beer and he takes me into his arms.

"Shall I put your address as the destination in Uber?" I ask him when our lips detach, my phone already in my hand.

I can now only see excitement in his eyes, "39th and 2nd," he grins at me. "Let me pay for the drinks while you order the Uber."

His studio is reasonably sized, and both his sofa and his bed are quite comfortable for our fiery thirty minutes, or so. He is as strong as he looks, even if not as strong as me. But he doesn't need to know this.

"I'm so sorry I need to go to work," he says afterwards. He seems like a good guy, but I will have to know more about him to learn more about the Professor.

"I will call you soon," he kisses me goodnight when we part ways at the 33rd street subway stop, where I go uptown to East Harlem and he goes downtown to the Lower East Side.

On the subway I text Shaila, "Thank you for Matt!"

And I text Jay, "Are you home? We need to talk."

Jay is not home when I get back, and only now I receive his reply, "Out with friends. Back in one hour. Are you ok?"

"Sure," I type fast.

Am I, though?

I have learned to live with myself, this new self who has powers, and stop asking how did this happen to me: I have put the words "the end" at the bottom of this book. I found my goal in helping the people who live in this city, because crime has reached a level that was never even in sight before. They're saying it's because of the economic crisis, or the last presidential elections which pulled out the worst from every single human being in this country. The Jehovah's Witnesses in the subway corridors say it's because humanity needs to pay the price for the shit we've been doing in the past decades, and now it's the time; you can hear them screaming that it's too late for us to be saved, our sins have gone too far. I even learned to accept the fact that I killed a man, because he was a bad man who meant just harm to the good people who live here. I haven't forgiven myself, though, because "good" and "bad" are still just ideals, like "hope", like "justice".

But now it seems a new chapter has been added to the book, which might provide explanations, give a meaning and a cause to my new life as a freak. Do I want to read this new chapter, do I want to know what happens next? Or am I content with the ending I read many years ago? Have I closed the book forever?

There are too many questions.

I fall asleep on the sofa.

36

WILD IS THE NIGHT
NEW YORK Pharmacy
3
Annalisa Conti

WILD IS THE NIGHT

"Guinn?"

I'm swimming in a sea of chocolate hazelnut cream, which sounds stickily uncomfortable but is actually smooth and refreshing, with the texture of the Mediterranean Sea in a warm summer day, and the sweet smell of a newly open jar of nutty delight. I can sip liquid chocolate, and I can also take a piece of bread and a knife from my bathing suit and spread some more solid buttery satisfaction on a toast.

"Guinn?"

A pink dolphin is swimming next to me now; he puts his fin on my shoulder in a fraternal hug, and he speaks to me with a deep voice and light Indian accent:

"Guinn, wake up."

I open my eyes, almost tasting chocolate and sugar in my mouth, and I see Jay with his hand on my shoulder, quietly shaking me to make me come back to life.

"Are you ok, Guinn?"

Am I ok? For now I have trouble remembering who I am, and why should I not be ok. The usual alcoholic headache tells me something about what led me to fall asleep on the sofa, still wearing my shoes, as I can quickly determine.

"I think I'm good. Are you ok, Jay?"

"You texted me that we needed to talk: what happened tonight?"

It all comes back to me in a flash: the date with Matt, the very hunky hottie Shaila hooked me up with; the satisfying conclusion to our short evening together; something regarding the fact that he had to go back to work to the lab…

"The lab!" it just comes out of me as I try to sit up on the sofa.

"What lab?"

Crap, my head hurts so badly. Why does alcohol have to have such a shitty effect on me? It is by far the worst side effect that came with my powers.

"Can you get me something for my headache? I can't think like this."

Jay looks at me, recognizing the drunken symptoms; he shrugs and heads to the bathroom to grab a bottle, taking a glass of water on the way back.

"Take two," he adds, handing me the open pill bottle, "And please tell me what the hell you're talking about."

"I already feel better," I smile my half-truth back at him, and I get more comfortable on the sofa, making room for him. "I had a very interesting date last night with this guy, Matt, who works in a medical lab. He runs tests on vaccines, some innovative types of vaccines mixed with antibodies. I didn't get much of it, but it sounded very cool."

"Are you talking about Professor Hoffmann's lab?"

The name rings a bell. How can Jay know everything about every mildly nerdy topic?

I nod.

"Professor Hoffmann heads some of the most advanced medical research on multi-clonal antibody therapy applied to vaccines," Jay looks really excited. "This Matt suddenly sounds more relevant than your usual… well, partners?"

"That's why I'm telling you about him! So he works with this professor, and he explained to me some of the applications their vaccines could have: personalized response to any disease, accelerated wound healing, regeneration of cells and tissues, potentially enhanced strength. Does it sound familiar?"

Jay has something in his eyes that I have never seen, a mix of horror and fascination. I guess my story on the Professor does sound familiar to him, at least as much as it did to me earlier tonight at the bar.

"Exactly," I add, reacting to his facial expression and adding a few decibels to the volume of my voice. "And brace for the most interesting part of the story. Exactly nine years ago, the research facility was completely blown up by a fire explosion. Matt didn't work there at the time, so he doesn't have many details about the fact, but he knows that our good professor didn't lose his drive or waste his time, and he quickly rebuilt a brand new lab to replace the old one. In the exact same place. Do you want to know where? Or do you want to guess?"

My mind rushes to that memory of nine years ago, to the morning I woke up with the worst hangover of my entire life, accompanied by some non-human powers that haven't left me ever since. All that after a girls' night out with an old friend of mine, hopping through bars that I can't remember, in the Lower East Side of our beloved Manhattan. Jay's mind seems to be working fast, as he probably runs through his own recollection of the story he has heard from me many times.

"I don't even need to guess," he says after a few seconds, a hint of sadness in his voice. "Professor Hoffmann's lab is in the Lower East Side, somewhere between Houston and Delancey, not far from the East River. He's on specialized newspapers every other month."

"Since when do you read specialized medical newspapers?"

Why am I even surprised? He reads everything and anything, from niche material engineering magazines to Vanity Fair.

He looks at me as if I was an idiot, "Since the day I moved in with you. I wanted to know what happened to you, I wanted to try to help you."

"And you never connected the professor's work with my situation?" I can't shut my mouth before I realize I already know the answer.

"I did."

Jay starts to cry. Just like this. Totally unprepared for it, I try to pat him on one shoulder, but the only effect this has is to make him sob even deeper. After a few long seconds he seems to regain his poise, and he looks at me straight in the eyes, a thin layer of tears still covering his gaze.

"I did. And it made me feel so frustrated, so powerless: I've been following this tiny light at the end of the tunnel for years, but it never got closer, it never got brighter. You're my best friend, and all I have been hoping for is to help you understand who you have become, what these powers have really done to you. The feeling of the Professor being connected to you has been getting stronger and stronger in my mind, but it is still just a feeling, a doubt, that I had since I read the first report on Phase One results of his research. It was published about a month after I moved here, coincidentally in the first number of the New England Journal of Medicine I ever received with my subscription. His rats were showing incredibly fast tissue regeneration after injuries, and I instantly thought about you."

"Because of the rats?"

Eyes wide open, he bursts out in one single laugh, before he decides to keep going with his serious doctoral tone.

"No Guinn, because of the regeneration. In these three years I have read all the published progresses and articles about his studies, to try and dissect the biological and molecular components that could have been involved in your transformation. It was really helpful information for me to build and then enhance your suit, knowing what your hidden strengths could be, how to enhance them, and how to protect your potentially weaker spots."

I shiver as my thoughts go to the many times I was stabbed and hurt, before Jay and I detected and correctly interpreted my weaknesses, and he finally perfected my armor.

I don't think I've ever stopped and thought about the work Jay has put in for me through the years: I've always seen this as my curse, but he has been dragged into it as much as I have. The hours of lost sleep designing my suit and looking for the materials that could bring it to existence in the lightest and most efficient way; the dedication to me and towards soothing my fucked up personality, constantly oscillating between sense of duty, refusal, euphoria, and drunkenness; the complete friendship, that never was scratched by my failures, my rage, my chronic lack of self-satisfaction. I am the one with the super powers, but I wouldn't be a superhero without Jay. I gently squeeze his arm, my silent thanks for devoting his private life to me.

I need to take one last thing out of my mind, though, "So did you know about the accident? Did you know about the fire in the Lower East Side and how this could be connected to the way I acquired these fucking powers?"

"No, this I didn't know."

Are you trying to protect me from something, Jay? My eyes try to pierce into his inner soul.

"Are you sure?"

"I promise, I didn't know anything about the accident! I would have told you. Damn, I would have investigated on it, if I had known, and maybe we could have done something about it."

For the first time I see fear in his eyes: he's afraid of me. He looks at me as the bad people I capture do sometimes, with a mix of admiration and horror. Then I realize I'm now holding his arm much stronger than I should.

"I trust you," I smile as I let go of his arm, which he starts to massage with a slight grimace. "But isn't it strange? I mean: if he's so well-known, why hasn't anybody mentioned the accident in one of your specialized papers? It would make a great American story of resilience and dedication to one's job."

"I have no idea, but I can do some research now."

He takes his computer out of his work bag, and in a few seconds he's all over Google, looking for old newspaper articles. I watch him and I can just think that I'm still a little drunk, that I couldn't do much without my best friend Jay, and that I have one more question for him.

"Why did you never tell me?"

He keeps looking at his screen, half focused and half embarrassed, "Because I didn't want to upset you: it took you such a long time to accept your powers and the fact that there's nothing you can do about them, beside living with them and using them in the best possible and just ways. I didn't want you to decide you needed to fight again against something, or someone."

"But the connection is clear: he's somehow responsible of what happened to me!"

"We don't know that: maybe he's just studying something that coincidentally could have similar effects. Maybe what he had done prior to the incident was not comparable to his current state. We don't know."

"Don't bullshit me," I spit back at him. "The connection is too clear to be a random one. And the fire happened in too much of a perfect place and time to be a coincidence."

"That's what we need to understand, Guinn: we need to find the truth, before we can act upon it."

I think I respect him for the way he always strives to be just, "We need to ensure that justice is made, right? So you keep playing with your internet, while I go kick some ass: it's almost two in the morning, time for W."

W's black suit spends its days in an armored crate under my bed, locked with an iris recognition padlock that Jay installed a few months ago. Every morning at two it comes to life, as I put it over my ultralight technical garments. I look at myself in the mirror, as I always do when I dress up: I see Guinn disappear behind my nightly alter ego, the normal woman hides behind the strong crime fighter, the personal assistant becomes a superhero. Everything is possible.

Jay has designed my armor so that it can cover up my female figure, and it has always been bulkier in some places, like the shoulders and the waist. But I notice something new in it: it feels more imposing right now, and the mirror shows me an even more intimidating reflection.

"Jay?" I call him from my bedroom. "Did you do something to my suit?"

He trots from the living room, his computer still in one hand as his research keeps running, "I inserted some new patches to reinforce it further against blades and firearms. I obtained some new pieces yesterday, and this morning I put them in place."

He yawns as I open my eyes wider and ask him, "You obtained some new pieces?"

He shrugs in response, and he goes back to the living room. After all I may not want to know where he did obtain those pieces.

My mind roams free as I run on the roofs of East Harlem, the sound of a chilly wind caressing my ears, my face and my body fully shielded by my black suit and mask. It's the best feeling of my nocturnal life: this sense of power and freedom, the smells of the night.

I keep thinking about Professor Hoffmann and how I'm more and more convinced that he screwed me with his little tricks. Jay is right: we need to find proof of his involvement, but all my mind can picture right now is my dark glove around his neck, my best threatening voice screaming in his face. My thoughts are interrupted by a clear sound: the radio that Jay has installed in my helmet has picked up some Police frequency, and I can get to work.

I can see you running in the dark, you two disgusting subnormal beings, chasing a woman who is just trying to return home after a night shift. You are the worst, there's nothing else to say. It gives me a physical pleasure to grab both of you by the neck, squeeze you hard enough to make your eyes roll, and feel the fear in your blood, just before I watch you pass out.

"Thank you," that's all the poor woman tells me, her voice still covered by her tears.

The lost look in her eyes inspires me to add a little personal touch: I strip the two idiots naked, I use their clothes to tie them up to a broken street light, and I leave them to their misery as soon as I hear the Police sirens approaching. Ah, the taste of accomplishment!

I run away from the dark alley before my buddies in uniform see me there, and I look for more action, before the lights of the day start to show up on the East River. The image of Professor Hoffmann hangs in a corner of my brain, and I try to shake it away by running faster. I swiftly move east, as it always seems that the closer to the river, the worse the people become in this forgotten neighborhood. I am not wrong: the radio tells me a Duane Reade is being robbed just a few blocks north from where I am right now. Fucking junkies. I hate them: they bring out the worst of me, they can always do unpredictable shit that drives me crazy, they can uncover my bloodiest killer instincts. I will never forgive them for this.

I pace even faster, to get there before they start hurting somebody. Pharmacists have my deepest respect: they see all kinds of weirdos, and they always have to keep it cool, half afraid of what the worst patients could do to them. I was getting some cold meds for Jay once, when a junky showed up at the counter, trying to buy opioids with a fake prescription and a jail ID. I could see the pharmacist struggling to keep her poise, and very politely telling the guy that unfortunately there was nothing she could do for him. I felt my shoulder muscles getting more and more tensed as each second passed, ready to jump in case I needed to defend her from him; luckily he was more tired than aggressive, and he left her alone, mouthing a curse of some kind.

To remain in control of myself and prevent my rage from exploding in front of the junkies, I play it safe, and I wait for them outside the pharmacy. I wish I could just enter, wave in front of the security cameras, and kick them all in their empty heads. They take their time, showing off their knives without realizing that everything is being recorded, and not even noticing that the personnel has already called the Police. Somebody will show up soon enough. The pharmacist does his best to stay calm, and to keep the assistants from freaking out. He gives some pill bottles to the junkies, who seem happy with their loot and get ready to leave. I stretch my fists as I wait for them next to entrance, no one else in sight for blocks. Junkies are so easy to surprise: most of the times they don't even see me coming, especially if they're still happily high from their last dose. These three are definitely not above average, which further pisses me off. They see me leaning against a street lamp and ironically gesturing at them, and they wave back at me with moronic smiles. They're hopeless.

"Such a good night, right fellows?" I do my best Deadpool impersonation, but I always fear I lack the fucked up charisma.

"We're cool, bro," one of them replies to me, evidently unaware of what is going to happen to him and his friends.

"Oh no buddy, I don't think we're cool," I reply as I stand tall in front of them, "Not cool at all."

It's the most frustrating thing to show my best moves to people who can't really appreciate them, so I decide to go for the efficiency, results rather than method. I kick the first one in the nuts, something that always gives me a quick delighted shiver, and I let him collapse on himself, hands on crotch, high whimpers from his crooked mouth. The second one suddenly realizes that something is off, and he tries to use his knife, sort of. I laugh at him as I pull the weapon away from his hand with a fast-paced punch, and I use my other hand to hit him in the middle of the face. Too bad for your nose, buddy. The third one is a woman, I hadn't noticed before. The best thing about being a woman inside a superhero armor is that I can be a true Knight of Equal Opportunities, and not really give a shit about punching girls. I even enjoy it when I see the complete surprise on their faces, when my open palm or my foot slams them down.

"Are you done here?" an unmistakable voice startles me as soon as I'm done with lady junkie.

"Chief Logan, what an honor to have you here in my office, please come in."

I open my arms in a very theatrical gesture, as the Chief of the New York City Police Department shakes his head with disgust, I believe both at me and at the junkies. He then watches with a grin of satisfaction as the three high idiots are being grabbed and carried away by some of his dogs, before fixating his angry eyebrows back at me.

"I should arrest you too, you weirdo." he charmingly barks at me.

"Come on, Logan, you know you like me, somewhere down there."

Too bad you can't see my grimace behind my mask, buddy. You looked at me in a very different way the first time we met, the only time I was not wearing my suit. My good old business consulting days, years ago: I was working on a high profile project for the City of New York, and my senior partner and I got invited to some holiday gala at the NYPD building. I was wearing my emerald dress, and you couldn't take your eyes off me: they were deep down my neckline, brushing against my hips. You were not too bad then, either: not yet the Chief, but a very successful Inspector, younger, less cynical, less fat, if I may confess. I would have let you screw me that night, if I were not in the first years of my curse. That was the time when I was afraid to let everyone touch me, fearing I could break them with my inhuman strength, or kill them. Too bad. You still have the same grey eyes, but their light is grimmer, and your whole body is getting more and more contracted, sturdy, as if you were carrying the weight of the world on your shoulders. And maybe you are.

"Fair enough, Chief," I finally add with a military salute and a bow, "I will let you do your job."

"Why do you do this?" he surprises me with a softer tone in his voice.

"What, the crime fighting or the irresistible charm?"

He doesn't laugh at my remarkable joke, so I hurry and add with a more serious and considerate tone, "I do it because I want to help this city, as much as you want."

He doesn't respond. Behind the usual rage and annoyance, a pale respect perspires on his skin. I think he likes me, after all.

I run away, before he can order his men to chase me. I climb on fire escapes to reach the roofs of my city, and from the top I watch over her. I look at Wards Island and Mott Haven around me, I perceive the wide expanse of Central and West Harlem with the corner of my eye; I know Central Park is a few blocks below, accompanied by the rich excitement of the Upper East Side and the quiet family life of the Upper West; I sigh when my thoughts go to the no man's land that Hell's Kitchen has become, and I wish somebody could do down there the same job I'm doing up here. Once again I feel I did something to help you, New York City, and at least a few of the people who try to survive every day in your dark embrace. I keep jumping from roof to roof, soon leaving 125th street behind me and holding the East River loyally by my right side, the first rays of a new day coming up from behind Queens.

When I get to my building's roof, I swiftly get out of my suit, and I slide down the emergency stairs to reach my bedroom's window, which I left slightly open when I started my night entertainment, a few hours ago. I put my W armor back to sleep in its crate, and get back to being just Guinn.

I follow the old habit and go check on Jay, to soon realize he is not in his bedroom: he fell asleep on the sofa, computer still on his lap and head bent backwards on the sofa's seatback. He looks like a child, skinny and lonely. He probably can sleep another couple of hours before he has to get up and go to work, so I softly remove the laptop from his hands' firm hold and I put it on the table. I take him in my arms to pull him up from the sofa, and to me he weighs less than his empty clothes would to anybody else. I put him in his bed and I half-close the door, my gaze leaning on him for one more second. Good night my friend.

I tuck myself under the sheets, wearing my sleep mask to get as much as I can out of the few hours that are granted to me this night. A positive side effect of my super powers is that I don't need much sleep: whatever Professor Hoffmann had in his hands when the accident happened, as preliminary as it might have been, it was definitely some good shit. I feel I'm about to drift to sleep, and I see an image of Matt in my mind's eye: maybe I'll call him tomorrow.

55
WHERE
TO GO
NEXT
4 th Stre
Annalisa Conti

56

WHERE TO GO NEXT

My eyes suddenly open in the dim light. What time is it? What day is it? Did I oversleep? I rub my forehead and I grab my phone on the nightstand, getting in a few seconds all the answers to my questions: it is Saturday, it is 8:13 in the morning, and no, I didn't oversleep for once. I sigh as memories from yesterday night make their way through my sleepy brain, and one name, yet without a face, pops up again and again: Professor Hoffmann. I scroll my head to clear my thoughts and I slowly walk to the restroom, careful not to make any noise that could wake Jay up. A peek towards his room reminds me how he must be already at work, since his door is open and he is not snoring under his sheets. After all these years I still haven't figured out his weird work shifts, and why sometimes he needs to go to the office on Saturdays. I suspect it might be for some special projects he conducts on his own account, like the ones that allow him to, what's the word he uses?, acquire new materials for my armor. I grin at my reflection in the mirror, thanking my friend for being a smartass in his own way. I decide to ignore the bad case of puffy eyes that yesterday night seems to have gifted me with, and I turn on the faucet in the shower. While the water flows on my face and down my body, I wonder what Professor Hoffmann looks like. Is he older or younger? What's the face of the man who might be the source of all my trouble? Jay would tell me to think about something else, and to remember that we don't actually know what happened on that night, a million years ago, but luckily or not he's not here to stop me today. Google gives me a good picture of the Professor: in his early fifties, grey-haired, not bad looking for his age, a certain harshness painted all over his face. Can this be the one man to blame? Who knows.

Shaila teaches a yoga class on Saturday morning at nine, and I decide to quickly jump in my pants and t-shirt to attend it, hoping for a mental break from my uncontrollable ruminating about Professor Hoffmann, his pale eyes now staring back at me in my mind.

"Look who decided to show up today, on a Saturday morning, and even on time!" my friend greets me when I step in the small room the gym reserves to her classes.

"Well, you know me: after great sex I always need some stretching."

I still can't believe my date with Matt, and its quite athletic conclusion, happened only yesterday night. It feels already buried in the past.

"I told you he was a good one," Shaila comes closer to me and she whispers in a low conspiratorial tone. "With that body he can do no wrong, if you know what I mean…"

"Are you sure you never went for a ride with him? Not even once?"

"You know me, babe: I can look at the menu, read through all the mains and the sides, and even the appetizers, but I never fail to stay loyal to my usual dish," she responds with a wink. I know her way too well, and I know her marriage to Marshall is the strongest bond a man and a woman could build on this planet. I still like to tease her, though, just for fun.

"Now grab a mat and get ready." she then adds in a higher voice. "Take example from Mrs. Grant, who is already stretching."

Mrs. Grant, two thousand years old and as flexible as a teenager, proudly smiles at me from a headstand. I will probably be dead way before I reach her age, and I am quite sure I never had her elasticity, not even when I was a baby. But that's life, and there's not much we can do about it.

A few more attendees come in, and Shaila gets us ready to start. As it usually happens, her voice guides me from pose to pose, putting me in a state of merciful hypnosis during which I blindly follow what she tells me to do. Standing, bending, twisting, laying, opening my chakras, elongating my back, reaching for the sky with one arm, saluting the sun with my chest pushed forward, closing my eyes and forgetting about everything. Too bad the effect is always temporary, and the spell breaks as soon as she claps her hands and wishes us a blessed and relaxed weekend.

"You should come more often," Shaila scolds me at the end, rinsing the sweat from the back of her neck with a bright orange towel. "The benefits of meditation would last longer, and you wouldn't go back to your signature frown so soon after the end of practice."

She touches my forehead with the tip of her thumb, her typical gesture when she senses my stress and tries to chase it away. Her perception is never wrong. I flaunt my best smile, showing off my teeth more like a hissing cat than a chuckling baby. She doesn't believe me for a second, but her next class is already waiting outside the door, and she doesn't have time to investigate further on what is making me upset today.

I walk home slowly after a quick shower. Layers of yoga-driven relaxation fall off me at each step, and when I push the apartment's door open I'm right where I started. Questions numb my brain and wild hypotheses make me wish I'd remember and understood more about that night, and I knew what Professor Hoffmann and his damn laboratory have to do with me. I give distraction another try, deciding to watch a new episode of something on the HBO app, thanks to the codes Jay kindly stole from his uncle. The TV show "Girls" is somehow the first item on the app's watch list, and I laugh out loud foretasting the moment I will give Jay a hard time for this. To be honest, though, he probably likes "Girls" for the sex scenes, the many sex scenes.

I binge through a good number of episodes, accompanied by a healthy lunch made of Tostitos and old cream cheese, before accepting the truth: nothing will distract me from my obsession today, other than paying a visit to the research center itself. I know it won't solve anything, but at least it could give my spinning mind something to maul, a bone to spend the rest of the weekend chewing on. I can see Jay putting his hands together and praying one of his gods for me not to do anything stupid, but it only takes me a second to shake that image away. I put on some clothes to cover the underwear I've been spending the previous few hours in, and I rush to the subway. I can feel the adrenaline pumping in my veins as I start this new mission. Sometimes I can't tell if I got addicted to the euphoria of the adventures, the action, the satisfaction at the end, and I'm not better than any junkie, who can't control herself and is ready to do anything for another dose. I certainly know, somewhere in the back of my head, that this is a bad idea.

Jay said the laboratory is in the Lower East Side, somewhere between Houston and Delancey and not far from the East River. That's all I know, so I spend my subway ride on my phone, trying to get more information. I'm about to get off at my stop, Spring Street, when I find an old medical publication by Professor Hoffmann where the address of his lab is mentioned as Ridge Street, with no number. I have nothing to lose, so I decide that will be my destination: I have all the time I need to explore the few blocks between Houston and Delancey. I run up the stairs and I emerge from the subway. I sprint through the mile of restaurants and cafes, so different in this bright afternoon than they are in my foggy memories of a long forgotten night. I trot east on Rivington Street, keeping an eye on the map on my phone to make sure I don't miss my turn. Norfolk and Suffolk go by, I can see Clinton Street a few steps away, and Ridge Street will be next. I am now legitimately running, my brain savoring the excitement of each molecule of adrenaline my glands are injecting in my blood stream, my muscles tensed and ready to explode into action, as if anything could happen right at that moment. I cross streets on red lights, getting honked at by furious cabs. I finally race left on Ridge Street, my eyes almost steamed up by my inhumanely accelerated metabolism. So steamed up and barely looking at where I am going, that I end up crashing into someone, and we both fall down heavily like rotten apples from a tree.

"I was hoping to see you soon, but I definitely didn't think I would meet you again this soon!"

Where have I already heard this voice? I have to remove a lock of hair from my face before I can look at the person in front of me.

"Matt?"

Fuck.

Ten million people live in this fucking city, and I have to meet the one who shouldn't see me here?

He takes my rage against my total lack of fortune (or is it Jay's gods savoring their revenge on me?) as surprise, and he smiles at me, offering his hand to help me get off my ass.

"Matt!" I try to have a less annoyed expression on my face. Not sure how successful I am, but at least he keeps smiling at me.

"Guinn," he acknowledges, as I'm now back on my feet. "Where are you running to?"

Good question. Think, Guinn, think. Where are you going? What are you doing here, probably ten feet from the research center he works at? Are you stalking him? Do you want to be that kind of weirdo? Think, Guinn, think.

"I'm meeting a friend for a drink a couple of blocks from here, on Houston, and I'm super late."

"Well, I would say you're quite early for a drink at this time in the afternoon," he shoots back with a grin.

Crap. I have never been good at lying.

I give a hint of a laugh, but I'm too embarrassed by my lack of creativity to find something more intelligent to say.

"What are you doing here?" I throw the ball back to his side of the field.

"The research center I work at is right on this block," he responds, then he points his finger to a brownstone building on the right side of the road, just a few feet north from where we are standing. Thank you for the information.

My brain somehow finds some neuronal connections, "Didn't you have to go to the lab yesterday night at ten? Did you just spend sixteen hours at work? Or did you have to go back again this afternoon? I mean, of course it's none of my business, but man, if they make you work for sixteen hours on a Friday night and Saturday morning I really hope they pay you good money!"

He laughs, the honest spontaneous reactions I liked yesterday night were clearly not the result of alcohol, but of his good predisposition to humor, "Don't worry, I didn't spend my night in the office. I just had to stay for a couple of hours to run some urgent tests, and then I could go back home. But yes, I had to come here again a couple of hours ago: I told you I have the worst shifts ever this weekend."

"Do you have to come back again tonight?"

"No no," he shakes his head in horror. "I won't let them ruin two of my nights in the same weekend. Sure, given how things went yesterday night, I would have rather spent more time with you and cut my friends' dinner short tonight, but I guess we can't plan everything in our lives."

That was cute. You hunky piece of cute ass.

Focus, Guinn!

Now I know two things: the first one, he's not coming back to work tonight, so I won't risk having to deal with him if I happen to roam again in this area later on. The second thing, he clearly likes me, and he could become my best source of information.

I smile and I flap my eyelashes at him, "You can always make it up to me one other night. Soon."

He comes closer, with a strange look on his face. My muscles contract, ready to face any unforeseen action from Matt. My whole body relaxes when he kisses me softly on a cheek, caressing my other cheek with the back of his hand.

Oh.

"For sure I will," he whispers, and he kisses me again, this time on the lips.

He then regains a safety distance, he taps on his phone and he scrolls through a few days on his calendar, "How about Wednesday night? No crazy shifts for me."

Wednesday night sounds great. Hell, any night is great for me: W's social life is definitely not that exciting. At least until two in the morning.

"I will text you with the details," he confirms. "And now I will let you go: you were already late for your appointment, and I don't want to keep you any longer."

My appointment? Ha, right.

I thank him and I wave at him as we part ways, heading north on Ridge street to pretend I have a non-imaginary friend to see somewhere on Houston. I slow down as I walk by the research center, manipulating my phone as if I were checking the map, and instead taking pictures of the building as I go. These will be useful when I'm back at home, to prepare for my little trip down here when the time is right, and the darkness can hide a black full-body suit.

I will have to plan Wednesday night very carefully, to make sure I get what I need from him, depending on how my little adventure goes tonight.

I get a bagel in a small random place on Houston, just to hang out long enough not to risk meeting Matt again on the subway or in the street. After a while I venture out again and walk back to Spring Street.

The apartment is silent when I open the door: Jay is still at work. I can take my time to run some additional Google research, since I need to have a better idea of the laboratory's interiors if I want to navigate through it, when I go back tonight. Jay won't like it: all his reprimands about justice, all his good words on how we don't know Professor Hoffmann's role in this sick game we're playing... Bullshit. Better, very smart points brought up by my very smart and sensitive friend, but the evidence is enough for me. And I'm pretty sure the evidence is more than enough for Jay, too: why would he keep reading about the Professor's research findings if he didn't think there was a clear connection, if he didn't think he could explain what happened to me nine years ago?

It's incredible how much of anybody's life is stored on the internet: it only takes me a few minutes to find some blueprints of the research center, published on the website of the architecture firm that was in charge of renovating the building after the accident. Detailed floor plans, locations of laboratories and archives, entrances and exits, I have everything I need to make my visit as effective as I can. A few seconds to upload the information on the operating system Jay has installed in my armor, to be able to visualize everything on my mask's visor, and I have just about the time to jump back on the sofa before my roommate kicks the door open.

"Long day?" I throw at him. "Need a beer?"

"Yes. And yes. But just one: it's too early for you to get wasted," he grins back at me.

A quick trip to the fridge and I'm back to my lazy post on the couch, Jay sitting next to me in our typical Saturday night catch-up configuration.

He swallows half the content of the bottle in one long gulp, before he can bring himself to say anything more, "I must have stayed up until four or five in the morning to do more research on Professor Hoffman. What time did you come back? I had probably just gone to bed."

I smile at the floating memory of his small body in my arms, as I put him down to bed when I found him asleep on the sofa this morning.

"You probably had," I nod and approach my bottle to his, for a quick cheer.

He nods and cheers, too.

"Anything interesting on the Professor?" I probe. Maybe I don't need to hide anything from him.

"Nothing more than what we already know," he frowns while recalling the last memories from yesterday night, before sleep cut his brain off. "I found no medical journals mentioning the accident at the research center in connection to the Professor's work. This is quite strange, since the center had opened a couple of years before and he was already the main researcher there, back then. It looks like he didn't publish anything before the fire; this happens sometimes, when scientists are so focused on their experiments to simply forget to write about them."

"Any newspapers mentioning the accident?"

"Not in detail: at that time, around summer 2007, there were many explosions in that area of Manhattan, mostly connected to gas leaks. The neighborhood was just starting to transition from its old shithole status to its current fashionable vibe, and constructions were ongoing on pretty much every block, not all of them exactly up to speed on the safety side. Buildings literally blew up in the Lower East Side on a weekly basis, and the local and national newspapers got tired of reporting the same news over and over again."

"What do we do now?"

Jay sighs, "I don't know. I could do some research on the laboratory personnel, to see what they were working on before and after the explosion, who was there with professor Hoffmann when the accident happened, who might have some proof."

Or I could go and take a look, Jay, don't you think?

"Sounds good," I gently squeeze his arm to comfort him. "Let's get something to eat and let's keep digging. Chinese from downstairs?"

He smiles and nods as he foretastes heavily fried spring rolls and pork belly, our usual order from Mrs. Chang's, sanitary grade pending in perpetuity.

It is the middle of the night when I peak towards the building that hosts the research center, from my hiding place between two bell towers of a church a few feet away. My adrenaline kicks in as I realize the small brick construction could guard the answers to many of my questions. I activate my mask's inner visor with a soft touch on a sensor on the side of my head, and the laboratory's blueprints pop up before my eyes. Will there be cameras? I will assume there will, to play it safe. Once again I have to thank Jay for a recent and very brilliant improvement to my armor, that will solve all of my camera issues. My helmet's radio has a very interesting additional feature that accompanies its receiving capabilities: it can also emit low frequency disturbing signals that confuse medium-tech devices like video cameras and simple alarm systems, preventing cameras from collecting and recording their images, and alarms from getting activated. The effect lasts only for a few minutes, since the functionality is pretty heavy on battery consumption, so I won't have a second to lose once I'm in.

I somewhat feel sorry for having kept Jay in the dark, but it's better for both of us, at least for now.

I stand up from my crouched hiding position, and I slide across the few roofs that separate me from the research center, as I turn on my camera neutralizing device. There is an emergency exit on the roof, and I gently push the door with enough force to open it without breaking it, glad that the alarm is under the influence of Jay's interfering signal. A count-down on my visor tells me that I only have three and a half minutes to leave the building before cameras and alarms come back up.

Corridors and offices on the last floor are dark, and the blueprints superimposed to my nocturnal vision guide me towards the stairs: the archives should be on the ground floor. I follow the red exit sign and cautiously open the staircase door. My boots brush the floor as I rush down: third floor, second floor, ground floor. I slowly open the door, just to close it right away when I'm greeted with full light. Shit. Somebody is here. The archives must be on the same floor where the urgent experiments take place, whatever tests forced Matt to visit the lab during the weekend. Shit. I try to remember what excuse Jay gave me for not installing a thermal visor in my mask, something related to weight or overheat. I will have to give him a hard time for this: I could now be surrounded by lab workers, who could see me as soon as I leave the coverage of the door and enter the corridor. What do I do? I didn't come this far to leave now. On the blueprints, the archives don't look too far on my right, while the actual laboratories seem all grouped towards the left end of the corridor. I will take the risk.

I reopen the door slowly, glancing on both sides to check for people. Nobody seems to be in sight. I take a deep breath and walk to the right, edging the wall, making no noise. I can see the archives behind a glass door at the bottom of the corridor. I reach the door in a few more steps, and, with a swift gesture to prevent the shutter from swinging open, I'm in.

What am I looking for? What did Jay say: we need to find proof of what was going on in the lab before and after the explosion, of who was there, what happened, and if they knew what they were doing when they created a monster. Me. I return to nocturnal vision in the dark archives, which are nothing but a big collection of books and files, and a few computers. I approach the closest computer, but I soon realize I don't have time to look for the password: my countdown says less than two minutes before cameras and alarms come back to life. I look for some order in the book shelves, and I get a hint of Professor Hoffmann's structured approach to his work: all documents are in chronological order. I rush towards the bottom of the room, where older papers should be filed, and I pace back in time through the early 2010s, then 2008, slowing down as I approach 2007. December, August, June. June 2007: that's when my accident happened. There's a red sticker on the shelf that separates events and records before and after June 2007: that must also be when the fire at the research laboratory happened. One and a half minute now. I grab the first folder to the left of the red sticker and I leaf through the pages, not understanding any of the medical lingo but taking as many pictures as I can in the few seconds I have. The reading and deciphering will have to be done at home. I rush backward in time through papers and packets, charts and tables filled with symbols and numbers. One minute fifteen. As I remove a thick book from the shelf, a loose sheet escapes, and while it's falling to the ground I perceive an image on it. I quickly take a picture, and the instantaneous flash of light illuminates the printed photo for a second. One second is enough for an alarm to sound inside my brain, about one minute before the actual alarms will go off if I'm still here. One second is enough for me to recognize those eyes in the picture, even among the four people who are cheerfully smiling around a younger Professor Hoffmann on the piece of paper I'm holding. My hand shakes. My whole body shakes.

I remember those eyes.

WHY ME?
5
JUNE
Annalisa Conti

74

WHY ME?

I remember those eyes.

I have always had a normal life. I had enjoyed my years in high school, where surely I wasn't among the most popular people, but neither one of the worst losers, a fact that had allowed me to survive through it better than other people. I had no social ambition in high school, other than making it through it as painlessly as I could. My only goal was to decently prepare for my SAT, enough to get admitted to Stanford Engineering and start my adult life from there. It still surprises me, sometimes, to realize how I succeeded: I was never the smartest nor the most zealous, but I had a fair combination of dedication and brains; I was not in any major sports team, but my proficiency in Vovinam, a Vietnamese martial art I had picked to honor my mother's origins, gave me the final little push that I needed to be admitted to the prestigious college.

The years at Stanford Engineering were by far the best of my youth: three years of undergrad, followed by two years of graduate school. In between, a couple of years spent working in one of those early tech startups in the Silicon Valley, in the first half of the glorious 2000's. Stanford was my place, the campus my second home, and I even had a boyfriend in grad school, the last serious relationship I could ever afford to sustain, before everything changed.

Towards the end of my Masters I decided, for some reason, that I didn't want to be an engineer, after all. Today I couldn't say if the change just happened, if I woke up one morning feeling I was done with the fabulous world of engineering. Or maybe it had been more of a gradual process, which I hadn't even realized was occupying my subconscious brain, while the conscious side of my mind was busy with equations, coding, and some practical laboratory experiments. What matters is that one morning I opened my eyes wanting to do something different, to interact more with people, rather than just with computers and machines, to give a chance to the creative Guinn, after so many years spent nurturing my rational self. Right at that time, I discovered the world of consulting. Business consulting firms were very cool in 2007, as I learned that spring from some former colleagues and classmates who had already jumped on the other side of the fence. Working in consulting seemed to make you feel entitled to tell people who were ridiculously more senior than you what they should do to save their companies. It sounded amazing, a perfect mix of bullshit, self-confidence, and creative genius.

The name on everybody's mouth was McKinsey. I didn't know anything about the company itself, what exactly it did, or even what business consulting was, after all, but with the brainlessness and determination of a twenty-five-year-old I dove deep into it. I spent a few weeks researching the company, its clients, the types of projects it focused on, the skills and previous experiences they were looking for in candidates. I polished my resume, shining more light on some aspects of it to nonchalantly keep other details more in the shadows. Given my Masters and work experience, I applied for a Junior Associate position, at which usually Ph.D. applicants are hired, thinking "What the hell, that's what I'm worth". I didn't send any other application: that was what I wanted. My friends thought I was crazy, as I missed all the job fairs at Stanford, and with them all other easy opportunities to make potential professional connections. I didn't give a shit. My boyfriend knew better than our other friends, and he supported me through the process. Or at least he pretended well enough.

Exactly one week after I had applied for the job on their online system, I received an email from the McKinsey Human Resources Department, in which a woman named Suskin was inviting me in for an interview. I grinned at my computer screen, mouthing a couple of curse words addressed to all the people who didn't believe I had a shot at this, and I responded to the sweet Suskin.

The interview was set up for the upcoming Monday, a sunny day in late May 2007, at the McKinsey's office in San Francisco's financial district. I remember exactly how I felt: I knew I was going to nail it. My interviewing skills had reached a master level through the years, thanks to the outstanding preparation I had received during my graduate years at Stanford, the practice gained while trying to get the Silicon Valley job, and my very charming and professional personality. I came out of the elevator marching on my brand new heels, copies of my resume safely stored in a slightly fancy computer bag, a smile towering on my face. I knew it was going to be challenging, but I also knew I could handle pressure better than any other candidate they could have found for the job. Clearly I didn't lack self-confidence.

The first conversation was with an Engagement Manager, a woman a few years older than me and two levels above the role I was applying for. She silently approved my shoes with a glance, before she shook my hand and invited me to sit in front of her at the table in the meeting room. A standard personal fit interview, it was more of a discussion rather than a test, and I used all my slyness to make her laugh, and think, all the way through.

Then came the Associates: a couple of years older than me, the two Guys In A Tie presented me with a business case and left me in the room by myself for forty-five minutes.

Thanks to my friend Tom, who had worked at McKinsey for three years and helped me prepare for the interviews, I knew exactly what to do. At the end of the forty-five minutes, the two Guys In A Tie came back in the room, followed by the Engagement Manager and two more senior people who barely introduced themselves. I was ready. And man, did they love me. I gave them everything they wanted, and I managed to find sharp answers to all their follow-up questions. As Tom had explained to me, business consulting was mostly a matter of applying common sense to complex questions, to break them up into simpler problems that one could easily solve. He was right.

My phone rang three days after the interview, as Suskin, the Human Resources lady, called me back as punctual as a guy after a successful first date, "Good morning, can I speak to Miss McGovern?"

"This is me speaking."

"Hello, Guinn, this is Suskin from McKinsey's HR Department. I am thrilled to inform you that the team had a great time getting to know you earlier this week, and they would like you to meet more team members."

She paused, soliciting my response.

An uncontrollable grimace popped up on my face, "This is great news, Suskin. Thank you for calling me back, I really appreciate it."

Very professional, Guinn, well done.

"Awesome!" the woman chirped on the other side of the phone. "The team would like you to pass the second and final round of interviews in our New York City offices. Would you be available the week after next?"

New York City?

Well, maybe it was a standard request. I took a mental note to ask Tom about it, and I scrolled through my agenda to check if I had anything coming up the week after next, the week of June 10. Once I confirmed with Suskin, she cheerfully told me she would arrange the schedule, and an assistant would be in touch with me to plan the trip.

I had never been more excited in my life. I could taste success and reward very clearly in my mouth. Plus, a paid trip to New York! I hadn't been to the city for ages: my family had moved from the Big Apple to the West Coast right before I started high school, and for the first few years we all kept going back to Brooklyn to visit my maternal grandmother every Thanksgiving. My parents and my brother Nick had kept the tradition alive, but I had been too deeply caught up with work, and later my Masters studies, to join them in the previous few years. The trip wouldn't probably leave me time to visit grandma, but it could be a perfect excuse to catch up with Stella, my best friend from middle school, who I had kept close contact with through the years.

It soon became apparent that McKinsey were going to interview me for a job in the New York City office, as they were trying to boost their high tech practice by importing talent from the West Coast. That opened the gates for personal questions that I didn't want to touch upon, yet: was I willing to move to New York? What was going to happen to the relationship with my boyfriend? How would we handle the distance, since his plans for the future didn't involve moving across the country, at that time? I parked those thoughts in a lot at the bottom of my brain, optimistically reassuring myself that we would find a solution together. While I was boarding my flight to JFK on that Monday morning in June, all my mental energy was focused on the interview the following day, and the success I would be hopefully celebrating with a heavy drinking night with Stella. Ha, meeting old friends has always been a pleasure.

It was baffling for me to see how much I could enjoy a walk through New York's Midtown on a sticky hot morning: from the hotel to the Museum of Modern Art, Saint Thomas Church, not disdaining a peek on Fifth Avenue, still mostly empty at that time of the day, and finally reaching the McKinsey building entrance just around the corner from Park Avenue. I was where I was supposed to be. And the best thing was that everybody seemed to agree with me. I met with two Engagement Managers and two Partners, in four separate interviews that covered a very large span of objectives, from evaluating my knowledge background and my problem solving skills, to discussing the Partners' strategy to expand their high tech business on the East Coast, to confirming that I would fit the team from a professional and personal perspective.

When the day was over, the second Partner, the more senior between the two who had interviewed me, came back to the meeting room and he regaled me with a conspiratorial smile. Without saying a word, he took his Cartier pen out of the chest pocket of his designer suit, he grabbed a sheet of paper from the pile that was lazily lying on the table, and he wrote down a number with slow, careful movements. He then placed his precious pen back in his pocket, and he handed me the paper.

"I'm making you an offer," he graciously pointed a long manicured finger at the six figures number that was seductively dancing in front of me. "That is the annual base salary. It is above the Junior Associate average, just so you know, because we think you have an exceptional potential. The performance bonus will be up to you: there is virtually no limit, high or low. I trust you will learn very quickly how to push it as high as it can go."

I would indeed, in the seven years he and I would end up working together.

After he left the room with a swift handshake, his Human Resources partner came back in to let me know that the offer would be on the table for two weeks. I would have accepted it right away, but I felt I had to honor her presence there with some mild negotiating, followed by some serious nodding and the promise to get back to her as soon as I could.

I left the office and the building with an aura of pride and achievement all around my body. My boyfriend was ecstatic when I called him to share the news, even more delighted than I thought he would be. A large smile filled my face when we ended our brief chuckling conversation: everything was going to be fine.

My afternoon was free, before my evening plans with Stella, so I decided to make the most of my stay in New York, since my flight was booked for the following early afternoon.

I went back to the hotel to get out of my business attire and change into something more appropriate for a young woman roaming the city on a warm June afternoon. I walked down Seventh Avenue to Times Square, to enjoy the lights and sparkles and mainstream shops; I walked back up on Fifth Avenue, pretending I had the money to look at fancy designer clothes and amusing myself in the fitting rooms of Sacks and Bergdorf Goodman. I kept pacing north towards Central Park, around the Pond, past the zoo, and I sat under a tree to finish my iced tea.

I loved New York: there was something in that city that had always fascinated me, even when I was a child and I used to live there, jumping from excitement to excitement across museums, libraries, summer events in the park and winter play dates in family friends' houses full of books. I was still under its spell at twenty-five years of age, already starting to see myself caught in a new adult life in the city that never sleeps, the place where opportunities abound and everything becomes possible. At that time I didn't know anything about the hidden face of the city, the one filled with violence and criminality, just a few blocks north from where I was sitting, and surely I was more dreaming than rationally planning for my future there, but I still felt that was the city for me. The soft touch of the wind on my face and the music of the leaves dancing on their branches were the only things I needed right then.

"Oh my God, Guinn!"

"Oh my God, Stella!"

We ran into each other's arms as soon as we recognized one another at our meeting place in the Lower East Side, later that night. I hadn't seen her in many years, and we both found ourselves imbibed in the joy of rediscovering each other, of getting to know again someone we used to know, of removing an old mask and seeing a new smiling face appearing underneath it. It was like meeting a new friend that reminded us of the old great friend we had once. It was a perfect night.

"You're so tall, Guinn! I would never have guessed you would get so tall!"

"And you're so beautiful, my friend," I responded, holding her even stronger in that first hug that we still didn't want to part from. "But I knew you would get very beautiful, let's be honest here."

We finally recovered from our mutual wonder, and were able to walk the few steps that were separating us from the small Turkish restaurant Stella had picked for the night. The Lower East Side was starting to come to life in those years, and Stella, always up to speed with the latest trends, knew which places were hot at that time, where to go to find the best cuisines and the coolest drinks. I can't even remember what we ate that night, even if my memories are very clear until long after dinner, but I was at the complete mercy of Stella's stories. Her life was a thunderstorm of events, people, places, discoveries, laughter. It was captivating, and she made me crave New York even more, if possible.

After dinner we started a whirlwind of bar hopping, meeting some of her friends in a new speakeasy bar in the Lower East Side, then sharing a drink just between the two of us in a small corner lounge bar, and later joining some other friends in a club. We ended our night with a stroll arm in arm, getting lost in the maze of lower Manhattan, chatting and laughing for a little while longer.

This is where everything ends for me.

The following morning I woke up in the darkness, my mouth arid, my senses numb. It took me a few seconds to remember where I was, as I started to recognize the details of the furniture shaping up from the barely illuminated background. I was in the hotel, in my bedroom. A sudden headache grabbed my forehead, as I noticed with slight surprise, since headaches were not my thing, not even after heavier drinking marathons. I tried to sit up in bed, but my head, spinning furiously around, told me that was not a good idea. Defeated, I laid down for a few more minutes, closing my eyes again. I cautiously groped around for my phone, brushing my fingers against the side of the bed, then letting their tips reach the side table and tiptoeing around to find the familiar shape of my mobile. The first question mark materialized in front of my eyes, still shut, when my fingers grabbed something sharp, a small piece of something hard and stinging. What was that? The piece was not alone, either, as my fingers kept capturing more and more similar fragments: bigger or smaller, they all seemed to come from the same source. I feared I had broken something in the room, maybe a lamp, when I had come back completely wasted. Maybe I had just drunk much more than I had realized. I slowly opened my eyes again and turned my head towards the side table: the lamp was still intact, so I clicked on its switch, barely visible in the dim light, to turn it on. The switch, one of those small pieces of metal one has to grab with two fingers and rotate, immediately broke at my touch. What a crappy lamp, I thought.

The only solution now was to reach the window to open the curtains and get some light from outside. Holding my head in my hands, to limit the painful pulsations, I slid out of bed. When I grabbed the curtain to thrust it open, the little metallic hooks that attached it to the rod suddenly fell to pieces, one by one, almost crushed by an invisible force. I opened my hand with horror, to let the curtain fall to the floor. A beam of sunlight had forced itself into the room, and I could look around: I was still wearing the dress from the previous night, but I was barefoot, my shoes broken on the floor. My purse laid on the armchair, its flap ripped apart and its chain decomposed into many segments. The sharp pieces on the nightstand were the ruins of my phone, now smashed and destroyed.

"What the fuck?"

At least my headache was slowly losing its grab on my brain, and my neurons could resume their working schedule. I went to the restroom to wash my face and retrieve my full senses. I broke the corridor and the bathroom switches while trying to turn them on, and I threw them violently away as if they were burning my fingers; the sink faucet knob came off when I lifted it up to get some fresh water; the cabinet doors broke loose when I tried to open them.

"What the fuck?!" this time I screamed even louder, the sting of panic stuck in my throat. It didn't help, but at least I could still recognize the sound of my voice: I thought maybe I still had some hope, maybe I hadn't gone crazy. At least not just yet.

What was wrong with me? Where did that impossible strength come from? I felt exactly the same, and that was my biggest issue at that point: something was obviously wrong, but I didn't even feel different, I didn't feel anything at all. The mirror showed me a scared face in the dim light, the eyes of someone who was completely lost, but deep inside my body there was no alarm sounding. I stripped naked to check if I had any sign of anything on my skin, tearing my dress to pieces and cursing like a fool in the process. Nothing.

What happened to me? It was clear that something did happen last night, during those hours now lost in my memory: I was walking with Stella in the Lower East Side and… Stella! Where was she? Could she know anything? I rushed out of the restroom, just to realize that I didn't have a phone anymore. How could I reach her? I could try to connect to Facebook through my computer, and message her, but I had to be very careful if I didn't want my new unexplainable strength to destroy my laptop, too. I looked around the bedroom, searching for something I could break without regrets, when I saw the already broken high heel sandals sadly laying in one corner. Using as much care as I could manage, I picked one of them up from the floor, and I gave a gentle flick on one side. A crack opened, but nothing more. I slowly grasped the heel with two fingers, sweat drops popping up on my forehead as I was focusing on controlling some muscles I didn't even know I had. When I felt I could handle the shoe without inflicting further damage, I grabbed one of the magazines piled on the coffee table. I slowly opened it, leafed through its pages, even managed to fold a page without wrecking it.

With slow and cautious moves I now unzipped my computer bag, removed my machine, and flapped it open. Like a surgeon in the middle of a ten-hour heart transplant, I paused and sighed, but nobody was by my side to pat my forehead dry or hand me a new tool. I started to type on the keyboard applying the tiniest of pressures, and in what felt like one hour I had composed and sent my message to Stella:

"Just woke up, I feel so dead! How are you?"

The laptop clock was telling me I still had one hour before I had to leave the hotel to go to the airport, so all I could do was packing, slowly and carefully, dressing up, and waiting for Stella's response.

It all took a few minutes.

"Super wasted!" she responded. "Don't remember much after the second bar – guess we had a great night!" smiley face.

Crap, that was not helpful.

"Do you feel good?"

"Hangover but good," she messaged back right away. "You?"

Me? Well, I could have told her that I had woken up with a superhuman force I could barely control, but then I opted for a winking face.

What happened last night? Why couldn't I, or Stella, remember anything? What was that monstrous force I now seemed to have? Monstrous was the correct word. Monster. Inhuman. Superhuman.

What had I become?

I spent the rest of my last hour in New York sitting on the floor, laying against the bed, trying to find some meaning in the situation, and in what I had become.

When the time was up, I left the hotel room, hoping they wouldn't notice the damages I had somehow tried to fix, and I caught a taxi downstairs to JFK airport.

Those eyes are the first thing to ever emerge from the complete fog of my memory black hole, the events of that night that broke my life in two pieces, determining a clear "before" and "after".

Where did I see those eyes on that night? What did I do to them and, even more relevant, what did they do to me? Why did they choose me? Why me?

WAY TO GO,
GUINN
Annalisa Conti

WAY TO GO, GUINN

Those eyes keep staring at me from the farthest corner of my memory, the same eyes that somehow pierced through from the picture I found in the laboratory, and that I believe I'm still holding in my hands.

It's like waking up from a dream: my muscles contract and relax again at my command, my eyes bring the scene into focus one pixel at a time, and I can now hear my blood roaring in my ears, as I slowly acknowledge the environment around me. Too slowly. The photograph is still in front of me, caught in my hand, but with the corner of my right eye I can see a red pulsating light, and it takes me a full second and two blinks to recognize the numbers of the countdown on my visor. Twenty-one. Twenty. I only have twenty seconds to leave the building before the effect of my helmet-emitted disturbing frequency wears off, letting all cameras and alarms resume their regular functionalities. I only have twenty seconds to get the hell out of here, before somebody sees me or something records my presence here, and I completely screw up this operation.

What do I do? Twenty seconds are not enough to run out of this room, make sure no one is in sight, cross the corridor, rush back up the stairs and leave the research center from the rooftop emergency exit. I need to think about something else. Quickly.

I scan the environment around me in desperate search for help from the room I'm in, the archives where all the laboratory's documentation is stored. I take a deep breath to free up some of my neurons from the stress of hyperventilation. While I'm thinking about what to do, I make sure I rearrange the shelves to bring them back to the exact state in which I found them: I don't want anybody to realize a visitor has stopped by. The movie-style excuse of "somebody left the window open and a gust of wind made all the papers fly around" would sound too stupid in this case.

The window.

I suddenly remember that I'm on the ground floor and I can leave the room through one of the windows. Eighteen seconds. I race through the archives, edging shelves and tables to reach the wall. I open the first window, throw a quick glance at the street outside hoping nobody is in sight, and I jump out of the room. I land on my feet on the other side of the window, dangerously close to the street, I shut the window panes as firmly as I can, and I look around. Fifteen seconds. Has anybody seen me? There's so much light here, as I'm standing right next to a freaking street light. In the Lower East Side on a Saturday night I might be lucky, and just cross drunk youngsters, or I might be way less lucky and meet a yawning policeman passing by. I don't want to make any fuss of my visit here; I would need to explain too many things, or to kick the poor cop's ass. Thirteen seconds.

I rush around the building to reach its back, where I find myself in a court illuminated by a small light. Fewer chances to be seen. Twelve seconds. I am stuck in this court now, though, since it is completely surrounded by other buildings. I gaze around me one more time, but there seems to be no escape from this trap I might have put myself in. I look up to the roof: if only I could reach the top and then jump back to safety on one of the rooftops of the bordering constructions. Ten seconds. A second light starts to blink on my visor, to make sure I am aware of the risk I'm taking. I know way too well, damn it. My only way out seems to be up, so I grab the first window cornice and then I grasp the drainpipe just above it, starting to climb on the wall. It's just three floors, I keep repeating myself as I swing and bounce on handhold after foothold, feet after feet, higher and higher. Spiderman would pat me on the back. Three seconds. The countdown on my visor is now doing the visual equivalent of a woman running and screaming in a horror movie, with multicolor lights flashing all over my peripheral view.

I reach the top of the research center and I leap over the roof railing, rolling on the roof and preserving the kinetic energy in my legs to keep running and prepare to jump to the next building. One second. My feet detach from the research center's roof as the countdown turns finally silent: zero. Did I make it on time?

The thought distracts me for just a moment, but my balance is skewed: I slide as I land on the roof of the adjacent building, slightly lower than the laboratory, and I roll disastrously on my knees and elbows, bumping against reinforcement pillars and knocking off chimneys. I freeze for a few seconds with my eyes closed, waiting for something to happen: an alarm to go off in the research center, a voice to scream, someone to grab me by the shoulder. After what seems like an eternity, I dare reopening my eyes. Nothing has happened, so far, and I can crawl back to my hiding place between the church's towers, a couple more buildings and a few more feet away from the research center.

I can finally breathe.

What a fucked up five minutes.

I sit with my back against one of the towers' walls, trying to bring my heart rate back to a decent pace, hoping nobody has a picture of me escaping from the laboratory building. I look at the sky and I see the darkness is already starting its transformation into dawn. I need to go home.

Jumping from roof to roof I follow the East River, all the way up from the East Village to my Upper East Side and East Harlem, where I finally land on top of my own building.

Glad we don't have any alarm in our rooftop area, or any camera recording my whereabouts, I remove my suit and helmet, and I hold them in my arms as I pace towards the roof's parapet. A few steps down the fire escape and I can reach my window and slide in my bedroom. Passing out on the bed takes me only one second.

"Rough night?" Jay asks me while he's handing me a cup of steaming coffee, a second mug firmly in his hands.

Even if it's very early on this Sunday morning, Jay is somehow awake and at his sharpest. I have no idea how he does it. I grunt in response: after less than three hours of sleep I can't really be more expressive than this. The coffee helps my mind recover, though, and in a few minutes I'm ready to face the consequences of my actions.

"I might have done something stupid yesterday night," I put my first card on the table.

"As Guinn or as W?"

"As W."

"Ha," Jay was clearly hoping I would go on to confess some drunken shag, but this is definitely not the case. He sits on the sofa and he gestures me to follow him; he leaves the coffee mug on the side table and he joins his hands on his lap, briefly closing his eyes. When he reopens them, I know he is ready for anything, his guru mode on.

"I might have gone to Professor Hoffmann's research center."

"And?"

"Nobody saw me," I want to put my one good card on the table, first, before all the other cards, the bad ones, with all the possible implications if anybody had actually seen me, come crumbling on top of it.

I still have to be honest with Jay, if not with myself, and I add right away, "I think."

"Let's assume nobody saw you and everything went fine," Jay pats my hand to calm me and bring me back to a more rational mental processing. He is the master of hand patting, like an old martial arts teacher from a manga comic book.

"What did you find out?" he finally asks, bringing his hands back down on his lap.

This seems to be going better than I had expected, so I let go a hint of a smile. Jay doesn't smile back. This is usually not a good sign.

"Don't be mad at me, buddy," I try to joke.

"I'm not mad at you," he very calmly replies. "I'm just disappointed: we had talked about it and we had agreed you wouldn't go there before we were sure of the Professor's involvement. Anyway, what did you find out?"

Jesus, Jay sounds like my father sometimes.

I open my computer to show him the pictures from last night, the numerous pages I was able to capture with the camera integrated in my W suit and that hopefully he can decipher, to identify some additional pieces of this truth we're looking for. He nods and points his finger at my screen, as he recognizes some of the names and topics in the research material. I keep the photo, the image containing those eyes that somehow emerged from my subconscious, as the last fragment.

"Let me show you the most important thing," I tell him as I double-click on my laptop's mouse pad to open the picture. Professor Hoffman's and four other people's faces appear on the screen, all smiles and pride in a memory from ten years ago. "Does anything ring a bell?"

He comes closer to the screen to focus on the five individuals.

"This is Professor Hoffman, a younger version of him," he starts, pointing at the face in the middle. "And these might be his closer collaborators from the time when the research center was set up. I'm not sure who's who, but we can look at the laboratory's publications: four names always come up with the Professor's on most of his articles, and with some luck they have all been with him since the beginning, when it looks like this picture was taken. It shouldn't be hard to match each face with a name. What's so important about this picture?"

I hesitate.

"I know these eyes," I then say, pointing at the person on the far right of the photo.

Jay doesn't understand, "How do you know these eyes? What do you mean?"

"I recognized them as soon as I saw them in the picture. They are the first thing that has ever emerged from the fog of that night, the night of the accident, the first and only detail I was somehow able to fish out of my subconscious brain.

Those eyes stared at me at some point, for some reason. I can't remember anything else, still, but this is the confirmation we needed, the proof that Professor Hoffmann is involved in this."

"Well, we don't know about Professor Hoffman, we just know Doctor Bellver is somehow implicated in this…"

"How do you know her name?" I can't stop myself from asking him. Hearing the word spoken out loud, being able to associate a name to those eyes, makes my muscles ache with anger. Who is this woman?

Jay answers my silent question, "She is the only woman in Professor Hoffmann's current leadership team, as well as in this picture, that's why I'm assuming that's her. She is also his closest colleague, a sort of right arm, and she has been for many years. Do you remember where the two of you met?"

I shake my head, feeling as powerless as one can be, "It must have been close to the research center, though, right? Maybe both of us were there around the time of the accident, maybe she even knows what happened!"

Maybe she is the one who did something to me, whatever happened to me that night. Maybe she is guilty.

I can't keep calm, even with Jay's healing hand-patting powers pushed at their maximum strength. Something clicks in the back of my skull, and I feel the same tsunami of hatred that had guided my actions in that terrible night when I had killed the junkie. The rusty taste of blood fills my mouth, as some animal instinct takes control over me.

"She was there. She knows something. Maybe she is guilty," I whisper. "I will find her, and she will confess."

She will suffer.

She will pay for what she did to me.

I can't think about anything else. I barely register the changes in my body, my hands closing in two hard fists, my eyes clouding over, my breath running faster, my heartbeat accelerating to above human levels.

She will pay.

Jay puts his fresh hand on my scorching forehead, and he leaves it there until I acknowledge it with a rapid eye movement.

I don't know how much time passes. He caresses my face to consume the overheating left in my system; I barely notice it, but it helps me slowly getting back to normal. I stare at him, not sure about what just happened.

"I guess this is a side of your powers we hadn't clearly analyzed, yet," Jay smiles and explains. "There must have been some aggressiveness enhancer in the magic potion you made contact with. Keep breathing and it will go away."

I close my eyes and practice some yoga breaths, in and out, slow and steady, until I feel I can speak again.

"I need to know Jay, I need to know why I am what I am."

He nods. He knows better than me how this is my real battle.

Jay brings me a tall glass of iced water to complete the process of calming my nerves, along with his computer to start researching our new target. He mumbles at his laptop's screen as I slowly sip the cold water, quietly perceiving the fluid as it rolls down my throat and freezes the revenge thoughts in my brain. Nobody speaks intelligible words for a long time.

"I have her story here," Jay finally says, sliding closer to me and placing his computer in between us, where we both can clearly see the web pages open on the screen. "As we already knew, Doctor Bellver has been working with Professor Hoffman for many years now, even before the research center was assigned to the Professor. She was his grad student, first, and then she did her PhD in microbiology and infectious diseases with him. Later on, she became his researcher, and through the years his closest collaborator. Just like the picture you found shows, she was there when the accident happened at the laboratory, and she and at least two other people in the photograph stuck with the Professor after the accident, and helped him rebuild his work from its ashes."

"This is all nice background information, Jay, but it's not really a story. Tell me something I can use!"

Don't try to bullshit me, buddy. I know you are trying to hold me back, giving me a small bone to chew, but I'm too hungry now to be content with a bite.

"What's her role in the accident?" I keep pressuring him. "Was she just caught in it, or did she provoke it? What does she have to do with the enhanced treatment I was kindly provided with? Where was she when I saw her that night: in the middle of the street, escaping from the building on fire? Or did she follow me and purposefully injected me with something? Was it just an accident? You can't leave me hanging in here with all these questions and no answer for them. I don't give a fuck about how she's been a great team member for Professor Hoffman, I need to know if she's responsible for what happened to me."

Jay sighs, his eyes telling me he already knows these are the questions I want to answer.

"These are not things I can find on Google," he then whispers, beaten. "But I don't want you to go and talk to her: if she is really involved in it, you could put yourself in danger."

Sweet Jay.

I laugh, "Jay, do you remember who you're talking to? There is no danger for me! What do you think she could do to me? I can kill people with my bare hands, remember?"

"She might have access to chemical agents that could interfere with your powers, for what we know. We actually know nothing about this lady, and she could be a crazy maniac or a perfectly fine scientist who has nothing to do with you."

"If she's innocent, we'll find out soon enough, and I promise I will stop looking for answers revolving around her. But if she's not innocent…"

"Then what, Guinn? Are you just going to kill her?"

"I'm not a killer."

"You're speaking like one."

Jay's eyes are locked into mine, as he tries to bring me back to reason. He always wins at the game of gazing, and so it happens this time, especially because I know he's right. Damn it, Jay.

I'm the one who sighs now, "But I still need to talk to Doctor Bellver and understand what's her part in this play: is she the main villain or just a second line dancer?"

"And how would you do it? You just go to her and ask her?"

"I don't know! Can't I just visit her in the laboratory with my W suit on, scare her a little bit, maybe shake her bones if need be, and see what she has to say?"

Jay looks at me like my mother used to when I was a child and I had done or said something really stupid, then he rolls his eyes, "No, you can't."

You're no fun, Jay.

"How would you approach her, then?" I sigh.

"We need to be smarter than her: she is a top class scientist, and if she is also some sort of evil monster creator, with all due respect to your powers…"

"Thanks, man."

"Any time," his politeness comes automatically, Jay barely realizes it. "If she is also the villain in our story, she's probably even much smarter than we think. We need her to reveal her secrets to us, to tell us what she knows without you using your force on her."

I can see Jay's brain mechanisms running at full speed behind his eyes, and I let him think out loud.

"We need to set a trap for her. We need her to do something that would clarify once and for all if she made you who you are now."

It all seems complicated, "Why do we need a trap? And what trap?"

He seems to suddenly remember that I'm sitting there next to him, "Well, as I said, we need her to reveal herself, because we've established we can't just go to her and ask her. But you're right, what trap? If she's guilty, if she created the modified antibody or whatever you got in contact with on that night, she must recognize its effects if she sees them. She must identify your above-human strength, healing powers, and enhanced aggressiveness as the results of her own work."

"And?"

Jay is thinking so hard that I'm worried smoke is going to come out of his ears.

"And if she is half as dedicated to her science as I think she is, she must feel she needs to take a look at the outcome of her experiment: you. She must want to see who or what she created, especially after all these years where she probably kept thinking nothing came out of her research, or at least nothing significant. I don't think she could resist the temptation of getting her hands on you."

"You make it almost sound sexy," I cut him off with a grin.

Jay looks at me with his eyes wide open, uncertain about my joke, then he shakes his head in despair before he can resume his line of thoughts, "As far as we know, you might be the only evidence of the success of her study, or whatever her research entailed, and maybe her only option to get out of the Professor's shadow."

"So we're back to square one: I'll go to her and I'll show her what I'm capable of."

"No, Guinn, as I said that could be too dangerous: we don't know who this person really is. No, we need something more subtle. She needs to learn or hear about you and your actions, and then we need to spy on her and follow her next moves."

"Basically I need my own Peter Parker to take pictures of me in action and send them to a newspaper, or something like this?" I throw out there.

Jay's eyes get all bright, "That's exactly what we need! Who is this Peter?"

Now it's my turn to have my eyes wide open and my disbelief sky high, "Fuck me, Jay, you don't know who Peter Parker is?"

He seriously thinks about it for a few seconds, then he shrugs quietly, "Friend of yours?"

I can't even.

"Peter Parker is Spiderman's real name. Do you know the comic book character? The one with spider webs coming out of his wrists?"

Please Jay, give me a sign of life.

"Oh, that Peter Parker," Jay tries to look less stupid. "Of course I know who Spiderman is. I thought you were talking about somebody you knew."

I can't even respond to that.

Jay tries to find his pride back, "Anyway, it's a great idea. We could have some photos of you published on a news blog or newspaper, and maybe even an article."

"Don't you think it would be risky for me to go public like this?"

Somehow his idea of danger is very different from mine. Somehow getting the whole world to learn about me and my powers seems less dangerous to him than a one-to-one chat with Doctor Bellver. Go figure.

"We don't have to say much about you: maybe just a blurry photo and a couple of comments from someone who saw you in action, like a passerby or a person you actually saved. They would just need to comment on how strong you are and how fast you can run, and stuff like this."

"And where would you find the picture and everything else? And where would you have them published?"

Jay winks, "I might have my own Peter Parker, after all."

WHAT COULD
GO WRONG
Annalisa Conti

WHAT COULD GO WRONG

"A SUPERHERO OF OUR OWN

A new hope has risen for the city with the highest criminality in the United States, in the form of a masked hero who jumps on top of the roofs of Manhattan in the darkest hours. Citizens who saw him describe the unknown person as "the fastest man I've ever seen: he caught the (expletive) who had attacked me, who was already several blocks away, in two strides", reports Megan, 73 years old, living in the Bronx. "He was stronger than anybody I had ever seen", adds Tracy, 29, living in Queens. "I think the robbers stabbed him, or at least they tried, and he was not even hurt", confirms Himanshu, 41 years old, a pharmacist at a Duane Reade in East Harlem. The consensus is unanimous on the masked superhero: he is helping the

Police in their thankless task of cleaning up the swamp of this city. He is arresting junkies and robbers, preventing assaults on women and elderly people, and delivering these criminals to the capable hands of our Police. Our requests for comments to the Office of the Chief of the New York City Police Department have gone unanswered.

Many questions still linger: who is hiding behind this powerful hero's mask? Is it an alien, as it happened in Metropolis? Is it a wealthy private citizen, as they do it in Gotham? Is it some sort of ancient God, sent to save us from hell and destruction? Whatever the answer, we just hope the streets of New York City will be safer now.

See all the pictures in the reportage on pages 3 to 7.

Join in the contest: how should we name our own superhero? Participate online or via text to 888-555-7777."

"They even have a "name your hero" contest, that's adorable!" I chirp to Jay as soon as I'm done reading the article in the New York Post.

"I guess the "w" symbol on the mask is too subtle: they didn't notice it from the pictures."

"Come on, it doesn't matter. I'm curious to see what names they will think for me: SuperAss? SexyWonder?" I grin.

"Why does it have to be sexual, Guinn?" Jay asks me, his eyes wide open and one hand slapping his forehead.

"Did you see the pictures they published?" I laugh as I turn the newspaper's page to go to the beginning of the photographic reportage. "They Photoshopped them, and in this one it looks like I have Brad Pitt's ass. In this other one they have enhanced my groin, and it looks like I'm horse-hung! In this other one they have pumped my pectorals and I look like The Rock," I keep pointing my fingers to the pictures while I'm turning the pages for Jay. He clearly hasn't seen the editing his own snapshots have gone through.

He now looks at me with a disappointed gaze in his eyes, "They assumed you were a man."

"Of course they did: wasn't it the purpose of the suit?" I smile back at him.

He sighs, "Yes and no: we wanted to make you neutral, we wanted W to be a symbol of all humanity, free of gender stereotypes, surely not a sexualized object on the other end of the spectrum."

"All I wanted was an armor that could protect me and at the same time make me look big and scary, and we definitively achieved that. I don't mind having a fan base of screaming teenage girls!"

Jay laughs now.

"Your friend at the Post was really fast," I change subjects. "You sent him the pictures on Sunday night and he has already published a full article."

"On Tuesday they always have a "local story of the week" piece, so this fits perfectly."

The trap is set now: with the pictures published by the Post, an alarm must ring in Doctor Bellver's mind. What will she do next?

"I am going to sleep now," Jay announces. "Don't come home too late."

"Guinn, wake up!"

What's going on?

"Guinn!"

"Jay, what the… what's up?"

"What did you do last night?" he waves his phone before my eyes.

"Why? What's wrong?" I'm trying to wake up. "What time is it?"

"It's early. I just woke up to go to work."

I can't tell if he's angry at me or excited: his breaths are faster and shorter than usual. I shake my head to clear my thoughts and my vision.

"Our plan is working," he's still talking. "Somebody took pictures of you in action yesterday night, and you're all over Twitter and Instagram!"

I look at the posts he's showing me on his phone.

"Is it a good thing?" I'm unsure.

"It is a great thing: the more pictures of you exist, the higher the chance we have for Doctor Bellver to see them, get interested in you and your powers, and accidentally reveal to us something about her past and the day of the accident."

"What if someone discovers I am W? I don't want to have this kind of trouble."

"No one will," he dismisses me. "You're too fast for people to follow you here. And my friend at the Post doesn't even know it's me who sent the pictures. I used a military-level encryption system to send him the photos anonymously. He has no way of tracing them back to me, not even the FBI would be able to."

He's so proud of his nerdiness. I squeeze him in my arms to thank him.

"Ouch," he whimpers. "You're too strong for me."

Sorry.

"Anyway," he resumes. "I'm sure something will happen soon, so let's wait and see."

"I have a date with Matt tonight…"

"Matt, as in the guy who works in Professor Hoffmann's research center?" Jay interrupts me.

"That's him."

Jay snorts. His mouth opens in preparation of a reprimand, but I'm faster than him.

"Calm down, Negative Nancy. I was saying I have a date with him tonight, so I can try and investigate if somebody mentioned the article and the pictures in the lab. See if they're getting all excited about me or if nobody cares."

"Is he even senior enough to know? Aren't you just going to get into more trouble?"

Jay asks, as usual, very pertinent questions.

"I don't know, but I guess I will find out," I shrug with a grimace.

Jay's morning frenzy brutally stole my sleep, so I get quickly dressed in my running gear and leave the apartment a few minutes after him. I run from our rickety brownstone to Thomas Jefferson Park, a few blocks away and right on the Harlem River. It's a beautiful day in late May, the fresh air coming from the ocean accompanies my steps, as I circle the small green area. My head is full of the workout playlist Shaila made for me on my Spotify. Its loud basses and repetitive lyrics help me keep the high rhythm of my run.

The day goes fast. After a long shower and a crowded subway ride I reach my office, where my brain is barely occupied by the usual cyclical repetition of tasks to attend to Mr. Sepulveda's sparse needs. I go home to get changed before heading out again to meet Matt: when I bumped into him on Saturday, he offered a date on this Wednesday night, and I accepted without second thoughts. Was it more for the ongoing investigation or for the still fresh memories of our previous date on Friday night? I grin at my image in the mirror: I can't hide that I'm looking forward to developments in both directions.

I pick a dark green dress, strapless, easier to remove should the need arise. Which I hope it will. I check my phone to find the date's details Matt sent me on Sunday: 7 pm at

Little Branch, 22 7th Avenue South. The man likes his spots in the West Village, conveniently close to work and not too far from his Midtown East studio. I like them smart.

On the 6 subway downtown I check Facebook for the first time today, as I'm not an avid user of social media. My eyebrows sprint upwards as soon as the first pictures and comments load up on my screen: W is everywhere. The neatest photos, taken yesterday night by I don't know who, already have thousands of likes and hundreds of shares. I indulge in reading the comments, and stumble upon as many "fake news!" as "this is the hero we needed!". It is always fascinating to see how people react to any groundbreaking news: disbelief is usually the first response, but soon enthusiasm replaces it and in some cases creates a form of social hysteria, a collective howling at the full moon. I keep scrolling and I read articles from local news blogs and posts from friends. I even find a video of me jumping from roof to roof, in an area of Manhattan that resembles the Upper East Side, dangerously close to home. Jay might have to rethink his strategy, or we risk having fanatics banging on our door soon enough.

I exit on Bleecker Street and pace calmly, my phone still in my hand. I don't want to get there too early and wait for Matt, that wouldn't be ladylike. As if anything about me was ever any farther from ladylike. I laugh out loud at myself, startling a girl who is walking just in front of me. I mouth an apology and I keep scrolling on my Facebook feed. I have to say W looks really hunky, even in the non-sexually-enhanced pictures published across social media.

I enter the bar and I look for Matt inside. He's not far from the entrance, a beer already in his hand and a second one next to it.

"Is that for me or do you really feel lonely tonight?" I greet him, gesturing at the second beer.

He turns his head to look at me in the eyes and he stands up to kiss me on the cheek.

"Definitely for you," he hands me the Stella, and we cheer.

He looks even hotter than I remembered. If I didn't have to wear my detective hat, and enquire about anything new possibly going on in the lab, I would call an Uber right now.

"How are things?" I sip my beer and I try to think about something else.

"All good," he responds. "I love this place, and you look amazing."

That's so on point.

"Plus, I don't have to work this weekend," he continues. "So I'm already excited about it, even if it's only Wednesday night."

A smile blooms on his face, captivating me.

Guinn, focus on the freaking job.

"No more shitty shifts at work?"

"Not this weekend, but they're always waiting for me behind a corner. The assignment I'm working on is a pretty long one, so I'll have to cope with it for a few more months."

"As long as you have some free time, that's not too bad," I look for the silver lining.

He smiles again, "I guess. But it's hard to spend the whole weekend at work and then have a Tuesday and Wednesday off: who's available to go to the movies on a Wednesday afternoon?"

"The only solution is to hang out with your colleagues," I put it out there. "At least you are on the same schedule."

My Stella is already dry, but I keep it in my hand to hide it from Matt: I need to stay focused for another few minutes, before I have another one and I get completely wasted. Jay still hasn't figured out why alcohol has such a bad effect on me, bypassing all my strengths and powers and what have you.

Matt doesn't immediately respond, so I add a second dose, "Are you close with your colleagues?"

"Not so much with the people who work in the lab, who are all much older than me. And all the most interesting people are like a sub-tribe: they have all known each other for many years and I think they have become friends with time."

"Who are the most interesting people?"

"The senior folks, like Professor Hoffmann, or even Doctor Bellver."

My heart misses a beat at the sound of those two names in the same sentence. The back of my head tickles with adrenaline.

"Does this Doctor Bellver run the lab with Professor Hoffmann?" I hold my breath.

"She does. They work together on most research activities, they have been for years. I am actually working with her on my current assignment."

My antennas get all buzzing.

"That's a "she" then… should I be worried?" I get closer to him and I brush my chest against his arm. "How is she?"

His smile is as naughty as my intentions, but my mind is fully focused on my target.

"She is older," he squeezes my hand. "And certainly not my type."

And what is your type, my dear?

Oh, come on, Guinn.

"And in the few years you've been working at the lab she or the Professor haven't opened up with the rest of the crew?"

He shrugs, "They don't hang out with the lab assistants. The only extra-office interactions we have are the social events the lab organizes every year."

That's a pity.

"Why are you so curious about my job?" it's his turn to ask questions. Luckily I paused at the first beer.

"I've always loved sciences, and after college I was convinced I would spend my life working as an engineer. As you know, this didn't happen, but I'm still fascinated by any science-related topic, and by people who work with science," I finish with a wink.

He relaxes and he leans backwards on the high chair, and I take advantage of the opening to rise up from my own stool and kiss him, standing in front of him. I hope this distracts him from my focus on his lab, and at the same time I count on not getting too carried away. Right. Should I use the bathroom escape to plan my next steps?

I softly wiggle out of his passionate embrace to excuse myself and check the restroom. This time at least I don't need to throw up.

While I'm looking at myself in the mirror, I think about the pieces of conversation we just had: is there any chance he could know more about Bellver's past? Could he be hiding useful information from me? Should I try to convince Jay to hack into his email accounts? Too many questions.

When I get back to the bar, Matt is hypnotized by his phone, and he startles when I place my hand on his shoulder.

"Sorry, I just got a notification form the New York Times app, and my phone buzzed in my pocket. Did you see this?" he asks me while he's handing me his phone to take a peek at the screen. His eyes are wide with thrill.

He taps on the play button on the screen, and the dark scene is set in motion: a black shadow is running in the street, fast and strong; it jumps on a fire escape to leave the ground level and climb up floor after floor; it lands on the roof and it jumps from building to building. The moonlight shines darts of silver light on W's full-face mask. I didn't know I looked this cool in action! A grin is about to form on my face when I realize the implications of it all: I am on the fucking New York Times. How many people will see this? How many people subscribe to the newspaper?

One word jumps in my head: national. Followed by a second word: international.

I'm so screwed.

I swallow a bolus of dry spit and I put up my best fake smile, "Is it a new movie?"

"This is real!" he yells above the rising music volume. "This guy is here in New York! Can you believe it?"

No shit.

"No way!" I play girly dumb. "It must be a marketing stunt."

"No, no, I've been following this all day long: an article came out on the New York Post yesterday night..."

Really?

"...and then videos of this guy started to pop up everywhere on the internet. If the New York Times is also reporting on it now, it must be true. We have a superhero in town!"

"I mean, it could still be a fake," I try to play my last card.

"I was reading the Times' article just when you came back. They say their sources confirmed the guy exists and he has some above-human powers. So it is definitely true now."

Now it's my turn to get suspicious, "Why are you so pumped up now? Have a fantasy with masked guys? Have a kink for black silicone full body suits?"

He laughs hard, "I'm not a weirdo! I'm just a big fanboy: give me a superhero comic book or any science-fiction movie, and you make me happy."

Am I just a science-fiction attraction now?

His face gets serious again.

"Plus, this is sort of what I'm working on."

Wait, what?

"That's the final goal of my research," he mysteriously hints, before gulping the remainder of his beer and ordering another round for both of us.

"What is?" my blood boils. "Creating freaks?"

My hand closes up in a fist. I have to slow down before I break something. Or someone.

He shakes his head while cheering with and drinking from the new full bottle, "No freaks: our goal is to treat all diseases, making humans stronger and more resistant. If this superhero guy is somehow more powerful and maybe even more resilient to illness than the average person, maybe he can help us make progress in our research."

Am I going to end up being the victim of my own scheme? Are Professor Hoffmann and Doctor Bellver going to kidnap me and run experiments on me? A picture of drills poking holes in my skull surfaces in my brain. I kick it out as swiftly as I can. I knew Jay's was not a good idea, and now the whole world knows about me.

"Are you excited, too?" Matt's voice shakes me.

I struggle to find words, until I get an idea, "It sounds really promising. Did you talk about it in the lab today?"

"Doctor Bellver is not in the lab this week. She's in Europe for a conference, but I will discuss this with her as soon as she comes back. I really believe this could change the course of our lives."

Me too.

"Should I get an Uber?"

Matt has been talking about W for an increasingly unbearable time, and I need a way out.

"Do you want to go home? Are you bored?" he worries.

I snort and I take his face in my hands, "Yes I want to go home, but not my home, and not alone. And no, I am not bored. But there are many other things we could be doing right now if we were home."

We kiss again, and he grabs the back of my neck, remembering the intensity of our previous post-drinks experience.

I smile at him, "So, should I get an Uber, now?"

This time he nods, still firmly holding my waist. Tonight he doesn't need to rush back to the lab to conduct time-sensitive tests.

Much later, I look outside one of his windows, a freshly opened bottle of Stella in my hand. I stretch my back and my arms. What should I do now? Just wait for Doctor Bellver to find me and reveal her responsibilities? Pay her a visit to put her in front of her faults? Risk being captured by the Professor and his band of mad scientists? No option seems valid. I'm trapped in this hole I dug for myself, stuck in a situation where I don't have control of what happens next, the worst possible configuration of events. I'm not good at waiting, so I will probably end up doing something, and it will surely be the wrong thing.

"What are you thinking about?" Matt emerges from his shower, towering in handsomeness.

"Do you want a beer?" I divert.

He takes it and grins, "One of my beers, you mean?"

"At least I'm offering."

We cheer and drink long sips, looking at each other from behind the bottles.

Will you be the key to my past?

WAY WORSE
Annalisa
Conti

128

WAY WORSE

Run.

I love this time of the year, when it's almost Memorial Day and the air is fresh at night. I love to take my own East River Express Highway, my route on the roofs, climbing and jumping from building to building. The view on the water and the sound of the wind rising from the ocean accompany my noiseless steps. I pace faster and faster on my way home. It's not dawn yet, but I can feel it coming in the smells of the city waking up, in the noises of the buses resuming their runs across the Upper East Side. I can't prevent a grin from deforming my face: this is my favorite time of the day. My night shift is almost over, and in a few bounces and sprints I can put W to bed, and go back to be just Guinn.

I reach 116th street. Here I need to use my Spiderman-worthy jumping qualities to cross the street and keep moving north: the road is too wide to just leap across it. I always pick the one spot where the building on the north side has had scaffoldings on it for ages, and large trees populate the south side of 116th street. Coming from south, I have to run as fast as I can to jump down from the roof, brush the top branches of the trees with my feet, and land on the scaffoldings on the other side. Every night I hope Jay is making some progress in the spider web throwers he promised me months ago. Or maybe he was just joking.

This night is not different, until I get to my jumping spot on 116th. I pause to take a breath and smell the air, before I run-up to the border of the roof. The moment my toes leave the surface, a lightning storm blinds me. I miss my checkpoint with the trees, my feet stumbling in the void and my arms whirling desperately in the air, and I crumble on the tarmac. I roll over a couple of times, to absorb the impact of the fifty-foot fall, using the sturdy gloves of my black full-body suit to protect my mask and my face.

"What the fuck?" I shake my head and I look around as soon as I find myself seated on my ass in the middle of the street, fighting to stand back up.

I still can't see anything, and I protect my eyes with my left arm as the lightning continues and it even increases. Only, it's not a storm, it's a herd of cameras, their flashes shooting without pause. Legitimate paparazzi.

"Were you fuckers waiting for me?" I mumble to nobody in particular, as I squint and I try to impress some of their faces in my memory, for later punishment.

"Tell us your name, the people want to know!" somebody screams.

"Are you going to save us or destroy us all?" a second voice adds.

"What do you want from us? Why are you here?" another reporter gives it a try.

I'm so screwed.

I tilt my head left and right but there's not much I can do, so I finally stretch up and I rush across 116th street, pursued by noises and yells. In front of me on the north side of the street there's a small space in between two buildings. I run through it, and now I can swiftly turn around the building on my right hand side and climb on its fire escape, all the way up to the roof. From there, I jump to the top of the next brownstone and then the following one, until I vanish from the paparazzi's lenses.

"They were waiting for me," I grab Jay's shoulder and I shake him, as soon as I slide into my bedroom's open window, and from there into his room.

"Who?" he is immediately alert.

"Papa-papa-razzi," I imitate Lady Gaga's voice.

"What?" he is clearly not impressed by my singing abilities.

"There were photographers waiting for me on 116th."

"W's 116th Crossing?" he opens his eyes wide.

"That one."

"You still haven't found another crossing at 116th? Are you still using the first one I told you about two years ago?" he sits up in bed, his facial expression an undecipherable mix of disbelief and amusement.

I sigh, "Man, don't give me hard times, ok? I didn't exactly have time to take tours of New York City to note down all potential spots where I can cross the wider streets. I have a couple for 42nd and 86th, but other streets are less lucky."

He smiles, trying to pet me a little.

"I will give you something by tomorrow night, a new crossing pathway," he squeezes my arm.

I sigh again and I let him get back to sleep for a few more minutes, before his alarm goes off. I barely hear him getting ready for work, as I snore my way to my own alarm, a couple of hours later.

"Help!"

A new night twists and turns in upper Manhattan, this one with the slight relief of the new crossing on 116thstreet. At least paparazzi won't find me tonight, until they discover the new pathway, or until they track me down at some of the other exposed crossing points.

I bounce on rooftops to follow the screams: someone is being attacked not far from where I am, in that unforgiving hole between Hell's Kitchen and Lincoln Center. I stop on top of an abandoned apartment building on the corner of 58th street and 12th avenue, and I can see two jerks gagging a family of four in an apartment on the other side of the avenue.

I shake my head: poor assholes robbing some probably poorer people. Where is this city going?

I throw myself from the roof. I grab an electricity cable loosely hanging between buildings, and I reach the fire escape on the other side of the road. The two criminals are facing their victims in the apartment, and they don't hear the soft noise the window makes when I slowly pull it open. I wave at the two kids to mean everything is fine, and then I put my left index on my mouth: silence. The robbers have guns. I punch the first guy in the back of his head, and he goes down like a leaf in November. The other one has a couple of precious seconds to aim and shoot at me, and he does it. Too bad his reflexes are nothing like mine, so I can easily avoid his bullet. One of my best moves. He's so startled that he can't act fast enough, so I just grab his gun from his shaky hands.

"Thank you, buddy," my voice roars through the frequency modifier, one of Jay's best gimmicks. I'm terrifying. I grin as I hit the guy on the temple with the stock of his own gun.

"Everything is fine, guys," I untie the parents, I absorb mommy's warm embrace, and I use their ropes to nicely wrap the two idiots who had broken into their apartment.

"Young man," I ask the boy, a child of ten or eleven years of age, to shake him up from his complete awe, "Get me some tape to finish the gift wrapping here. And call 911: there's a package for them."

"Hello my friends," I jump down the fire escape and I greet the two cops when they get out of their car a few minutes later, in front of the building. Two familiar faces I had already offered my presents to many times.

"Third floor. I wish I had a bow, but I hope you don't mind if the wrapping is a bit unconventional," I grin, so proud of my sense of humor.

They don't laugh. They never do, but this time something seems odd.

"All units, we have a code seventy-seven here. 58th street and 12th avenue," Lady Cop mumbles in her radio, taking her gun out.

Guy Cop points his gun at me, "Put your hands where I can see them."

"Ha ha, you're making a joke. I didn't know you guys knew jokes! This is funny."

Lady Cop takes the safety catch off her gun, and she holds it with her two hands as she keeps pointing it at me, "Put your hands where I can see them."

"What's the problem, guys?" I try to play it cool.

They keep looking at me, small drops of sweat forming on the sides of their heads. Their guns don't move, and I start slowly putting my hands above my head.

"Come on," I don't give up, "You know me, guys. I mean, we haven't been out on an official date, yet, but I saved your asses at least a couple of times."

They look at each other. They hesitate for one long second, before Lady Cop sighs, "New orders: we have to arrest you."

I try to laugh, but she is dead serious.

"What the fuck?" I can't believe it.

"Directly from the Office of the Chief," Guy Cop explains, embarrassed.

Damn it, Chief Logan, what's wrong with you?

"Come on, guys, why would the Chief want you to arrest me?" this doesn't make any sense.

They lower their guns and they snort in unison. So cute.

Lady Cop explains, "Chief Logan is really pissed off: with all your videos and crap all around the internet, you're making him look like an asshole. How can he still claim he can do his job, if there's this idiot in a black leotard who roams on the roofs of his city, undisturbed, with unclear intentions and a secret identity? No offence."

"None taken, ma'am," I reassure her with a bow. "But I'm not the one putting that shit on Facebook, right? There's nothing I can do about it. And I would never want the NYPD to look like assholes: you know I love you guys. I've been quite a good little helper for Santa Logan, so far."

"We know," Guy Cop agrees, "But the Chief has to save his face and the reputation of the whole department. Those jerks at the New York Post have already published a couple of satirical cartoons about him, and trust me, he was not happy. So the order came out."

Crap.

"Go, before I change my mind," Lady Cop puts her gun away with a sigh and a grimace. "We'll tell our colleagues you ran away before we could arrest you. But everybody is looking for you."

"Watch out," Guy Cop adds, before they enter the building to grab the robbers and collect the family's deposition.

What do I do now?

I am sitting on my own fire escape. W's suit already hides in its case under my bed, Guinn's plain clothes are back in action, as the moon is shining on my thoughts.

"What are you doing here so early?" Jay peeks in. "I heard some noises in here and I feared photographers had found us…"

"That's even worse," I sigh as I get ready to share with him the latest developments of the situation.

"I'm so sorry," he says in the end. "I didn't think this would happen."

"What do I do now? With paparazzi following me and the Police chasing me, how do I get around at night?"

"I guess you will have to lay low for some time," he carefully suggests, as if he had in fact already thought about it.

I climb into the window to get inside my bedroom and I look at Jay, "I guess we can have a beer then."

We only have one each, because he has to go to work tomorrow and his alarm always goes off at some unlikely time. One beer is not enough to get me drunk, but I still text Matt as soon as Jay goes off to bed. If I need to lay low, I might as well use my night time in a more profitable way. Who needs to sleep anyway?

"Still awake?"

To my surprise, he responds right away, "Leaving work now."

Perfect timing.

"Did you have a good day so far?" I test the water.

"Have you seen the latest videos of the superhero? My Twitter feed is monopolized by this guy!" he responds, instead.

The next thing I know, he sends me link after link to YouTube videos of… well, of myself vaulting on the roofs, climbing on scaffoldings and fire escapes, in some scenes dangerously close to home. He even sends me a new article the New York Times has just published about the "unnamed superhero (or super criminal?) who animates our late nights".

I mouth a curse word. Enough with W already.

"No, I hadn't seen all these new videos. Just wanted to say hi, I'm off to bed," I type as quickly as I can, and I turn my phone off.

There's only one thing I want to do right now: drink. But not alone.

I put on some jeans and a decently looking top and I leave the apartment, grabbing my purse on the way out. As I walk to the subway's downtown entrance, I think about where can I go: Lower East Side? Too far. West Village? Not on a week-night. Upper West Side? Too preppy. Hell's Kitchen? It will do.

I get off my train at 50th street and I ask for a beer in the first appropriate bar I find on 8th avenue: moderately sketchy, and an alcohol smelling intensity I can still manage.

Halfway through my beer, the first guy approaches me with the classic "Is this seat taken?" move, directly from 'How to hook up with women in bars, volume one'. Saying that I hadn't even seen him is not mild enough to describe his dullness.

I burn him alive with a glance.

He seems to get the message, as he strategically retreats to his background table.

I ask the bartender for a second beer, and another guy offers to pay for it.

"This one is one me, babe," he says.

Images of my left punch landing in the exact middle of his eyes fly in my brain, but I apply myself to being polite and I decline the offer with a very much fake smile.

That's when he makes his mistake: he bloody insists.

"Oh, come on. What are you, too precious of a flower to accept a beer? Did you want a Cosmopolitan? Bitch."

Oh, man.

Before I realize what I'm doing, I stand up and I grab him by his balls. Literally.

"Who's the flower now, bitch?" I whisper in his ear.

The fear in his eyes makes me smile, as I squeeze his actually quite small privates just a little tighter. He squeals.

"That's what I thought," I chuckle.

I let him go and he runs away, whimpering.

"That was impressive," yet another guy sits next to me at the bar.

I sigh so heavily that a wheeze comes out of my throat, too. I throw my best shade at him, before realizing this one is at least good-looking.

"Woah," he puts his open palms up to protect himself, "Please don't grab my balls, too."

I give a hint of a smile, "Yeah, you wouldn't want that," I nod.

"I mean, not in that way," he grins.

"Definitely not in that way," I confirm.

He throws his hand out, "My name is Zack."

"Ok."

"I'm a cop," he adds.

"Shit," I tell myself.

"Is that always the first thing you say when you meet a girl in a bar, 'I'm a cop'? Do you like them scared?" I ask.

He laughs, "I always thought it was a good move."

My eyes open wide as my eyebrows jump to the roof, "You thought it was a good move? Where the fuck did you find it, on 'How to never get laid, volume one'? Sure that shit works."

He laughs again, "Some women like cops."

"Right, and some men like anal plugs."

He laughs harder.

"I'm sorry, maybe you like anal plugs yourself?" I fake concern.

He takes his head in his hands and he seems not to be able to stop laughing. Are my jokes that good? Or is it lesson number two in his manual: 'Let her believe she's smart'?

When he finally finds his poise back, he keeps smiling, "Man, you're something!"

"What kind of cop are you?"

"Detective."

Hopefully you're not investigating W, detective.

"Were you following me?" I keep joking.

"You got me. I had a lead on a ball-grabbing woman terrorizing Hell's Kitchen."

"Yep, that would be me then," I stand up from the barstool and I give him my wrists. "Arrest me, officer, I'm guilty."

He grabs my wrists and he pulls me closer to him. This is one of those situations where I am thankful for my life-screwing powers: I have nothing to fear. He could be an

Olympic gold medal wrestler, and he wouldn't be able to pinch me. He could have a gun in his pocket, and he wouldn't have the time to take it out and point it at me. Hooking up in bars and blind dating through apps would have never been my weapon of choice, if I hadn't been cursed with my inhuman powers.

He whispers in my ear, "I will have to bring you in for questioning."

"To the precinct?" I pose with naivety.

He pulls me closer.

"The precinct is quite far from here, unfortunately, and I have a feeling you might attempt an escape from custody. I wouldn't want you to get away with what you did without a proper punishment."

He winks, "My apartment is only a few blocks from here."

I free myself up from his embrace, as I don't want to make things too easy for him.

"Well, detective, let's see if you can convince me."

A few hours later, I sneak through my bedroom's open window into my apartment, and I see Jay rolling down the corridor from his room to the bathroom. Is it already time for him to go to work? Detective Zack must have been more entertaining than I thought.

"Didn't we say it was a good idea to lay low for a while?" Jay sighs.

"We did," I grin.

"Then, where have you been?"

"I had a close encounter with a NYPD detective…"

"What happened?" he now looks legitimately concerned.

A larger smile pops up on my face. Adorable Jay.

"Do you want to know all the details?" I wink.

He now starts to grasp the context of my engagement with the police, and he frowns, even more surprised, "As W?"

"Come on, Jay! Think, McFly, think!" I lightly tap my fist on his head. "No, not as W, as Guinn. Don't you think it would have been a bit too hard to have sex with my armor on?"

He is not impressed and he shakes his head, "Not for you."

I look for something to say, but he leaves me hanging in the corridor, my mouth open, my brain trying to come up with a new joke to throw in the mix.

"Since you need to let W rest for at least a few weeks, you should focus on finding a better way to use your nighttime," he yells from behind the bathroom's closed door. "Rather than hooking up with strangers in bars.

I don't see what's wrong with enjoying my fading thirties, but fair point, I guess. I shrug and I walk back to my room, hoping I can catch two hours of sleep before I have to go to work, too. I'll plan for a better me tomorrow.

Maybe.

WORK HARD, PLAY HARDER

WORK HARD, PLAY HARDER

In my dream I'm dead.

It's one of those strange dreams where all is blurry, I can't recognize faces and I don't really know what's going on, but I know I'm dead. It's a weird feeling, being dead. There's some sort of quiet, a resignation that comes with it: you did what you could, and now it's over.

The alarm goes off at eight, like every other day. My two hours of sleep flew by way too fast. I open my eyes in the blinding light of a mid-June Wednesday morning, to the sound of the humming fan in my room. Why doesn't this damn thing do anything, it's so fucking hot in here. I listen to the noises in the apartment: water running in the pipes, footsteps above my head, cars honking outside the window, a woman yelling some unintelligible words in the street. East Harlem is already awake. I'm alone in here. Jay always leaves early to go to his job in New Jersey, where he spends his days playing with innovative materials for the military.

Images from yesterday night come to the surface of my mind: a bar and a drink with Matt, sweet Matt, incredibly hot Matt. A ride home on the back seat of an Uber, clutching each other with lust more than affection. A few hours together in his apartment. I sigh. At least now he's slightly less focused on W, as there have been no new pictures or videos in a few weeks. I have been forced to take a vacation from my other identity, to escape both the paparazzi and my buddy Police Chief Logan and his boys. I scratch my head. Am I remembering yesterday night correctly? Did I decide not to go home after I left Matt's apartment? Did I somehow end up in that bar in Hell's Kitchen, still drunk after the two more beers I had at Matt's? Everything is a blur.

I crawl to the bathtub, where I turn the shower knob to spray fresh water on my face, hoping to find some clarity. I hate how alcohol can drag me down, while nothing else can physically hurt me. Memories start to come back, as cold needles hit my skin. I actually went to the bar in Hell's Kitchen, hoping to get another drink, drown my thoughts and numb my brain for a little longer. There, Detective Zack showed up again, making all the alarms in my head explode with noises and lights.

"Man, I haven't been here in weeks, and now you show up?" I greeted him.

I don't even remember what he replied, but it must have been good enough to drag me in his bed again. Rivers roll down my cheeks and my neck, falling all the way to the bottom of the bathtub. I sigh again. I am an adult and I know I have done nothing to be ashamed of, but shame is a strange slimy thing. It itches in my chest, and as much as I slam it down it keeps crawling up from my feet. Jay wouldn't be proud of how I'm using my nights, but there's nothing else I'd rather do. Sometimes I wish we could all remain children all our life, and forget our faults in the time of a breath.

On the 6 train nobody looks at me: I'm tall, but I'm just another skinny vaguely Vietnamese-looking girl in a ponytail. They are all too busy checking their phones, their Facebook pages, their Twitters. But I see them all, I look at them, I spy behind their masks: will I see you one night in a black alley? Will I have to smash your head against a wall? Long gone are the times when I had to pay attention not to touch anybody, afraid of hurting people with my new powers. Things are easier now: I just need to remember to get off the train at Grand Central, to go to work.

"Good morning, Guinn!" Tony Sepulveda arrives a couple of minutes after me, and he catches me at my desk while I'm printing out his schedule for the day.

"I finalized your speech for tomorrow's earnings call," I tell him as I walk with him to his office, a cup of coffee for him in my hand.

"Did you leave the celebratory part in?" he investigates.

"In the end, I did. I think it makes sense for you, as the President, to showcase the company's major client achievements of the past quarter. It's true that your son is now the CEO, but he can still talk about future developments, like how the contracts he just signed with Delta and Pepsi for their next Super Bowl's campaigns will impact our topline."

"And Jeff can run his show?" Tony winks, referring to the Chief Financial Officer of his global advertising company.

I laugh and I nod, "Jeff can juggle his financials balls as usual. The Street will love the increase in Earnings per Share, and forget to listen about anything else."

Tony looks at me straight in the eyes for one long second, with a half-smile on his face, "Sometimes I get the feeling you could run the place without me."

I grin back at him, "Don't say it twice…"

"But I mean it, with your degrees from Stanford and the rest of your resume! Are you sure you don't want me to find another role for you? You've been my executive assistant for two years: it's time to move if you want to."

"But I don't want to. I'm perfectly fine where I am, and you know it."

This job lets my brain and my body rest after my sleepless nights. Be it W's or alcohol's fault, I always manage not to get enough sleep. I couldn't do anything more challenging, not at this point: I need a simple job that pays my rent and lets me snooze after lunch. After all, Tony snoozes after lunch most days, too.

"You tell me the minute you change your mind, ok?"

"Ok," I respond as I leave his office to reach my own room, next to his.

A tangled heaviness possesses me today. My eyes have been staring at Tony's Outlook calendar for I don't know how long after lunch, and the characters "June 15" have left a permanent mark on my retinas. I take my head in my hands and I squeeze my eyes to look for my lost focus, trying to resist the urge to bang my forehead on the computer's keyboard.

I switch to something else, and I decide to proof-read tomorrow's speech for the tenth time. After the first sentence, words start floating on the page I'm holding in my hands, laughing at me and my ineptitude. If there's one thing I've never lacked is self-confidence, but today is not my best day. Each paragraph reads worse than the other, I struggle to understand the meaning of my own phrases, and for the first time in a long time I feel incapable, useless.

What the hell is wrong with me?

I drink a Coke. I actually drink a Pepsi, since now they're our clients.

Caffeine helps, and I can stumble myself through the rest of my day.

It's dark outside when I leave the office. The suffocating heat of the morning has given its seat to a humid afternoon, and a gray rain falls on my head while I walk to Grand

Central Station. I find myself on the platform, waiting for my 6 train home, my eyes lost in the void of the subway tunnel.

The noise of my phone vibrating in my purse uproots me from the pit of my own thoughts, "Hey."

Jay's relationship with texts has always been less than amicable.

"Hey," I type with one finger.

"Got beer at home?"

"Dunno," but it's the right question to ask. A beer could help me feel less useless tonight, or at least forget about it.

"Ok, I'll stop on the way home to buy some."

"Good boy Jay."

I get home and I sit on the couch. I don't move, I barely breathe, I listen to the noises of my heart against my rib cage. I just stay there, I contemplate the void in front of me, and I stare at the emptiness of my soul inside me. Now I'm alone and there's nothing stopping me from looking at myself. What am I doing? I keep repeating these words in my head: what am I doing? I decided to use my powers to help the people in this city, because crime had reached unbelievable heights. I used to think that New York City could be saved, that maybe I could do something to save it, but now I don't know anymore. I don't know if I'm worth it anymore: what hero gets scared by paparazzi? What hero gets distracted by the simple fact that the police is looking for them? Maybe I'm not a hero, not anymore. Or maybe I never was. The plague of perdition that is spreading in this city has already infected me: alcohol and sex and bars occupied my mind and my body in the past few weeks, while I was too scared to do my job. To be W. Can I be saved? Can I be redeemed?

The key turns in the lock, and I can glimpse with the corner of my eye Jay entering our apartment. I don't want to look at him, I don't want to recognize on his face the disappointment, the frustration he has to fight every time I get home drunk and lost. I know he stares at me, and with a gaze he understands that I haven't moved since I came home from work. My bag is on the carpet, my shoes are still on my feet.

He takes a beer out of a brown paper bag I hadn't noticed, he opens the twist cap and he hands it to me; he takes one for himself, "Cheers."

The bottles clink and the sound wakes me up from my silent exile, "Cheers."

"So you can speak," he notices with a smile, which vanishes rapidly as he watches me drink my beer in one long sip.

"Another one," I let the empty bottle slide on the floor, careless. Good thing he bought two six-packs.

I need to drink two more before I'm ready to talk, and he knows it.

"How are you?" he asks.

"Are you fucking kidding me?" I respond with a burp.

"Well, I know you feel like shit, but what do you want me to say?"

"Oh, you know I feel like shit?"

Jay sighs, "Yes. Do you know when was the last time you had that look on your face?"

I shake my head.

"The morning after… well, the morning after the accident with the junkie, a few months back."

Oh.

"You mean, the day I killed a man?" I challenge him.

He can't face my gaze and he looks down to his hands in his lap, "That day."

Silence rumbles.

"We haven't talked about it in quite some time," he says after a while.

I nod.

"Do you want me to tell you again what I think?" he offers.

The alcohol speaks for me, "I don't know: that I'm a monster and you don't want to be my friend anymore?"

"No, and no. You're not a monster and you're my best friend, so stop acting like a child."

"Ok, your High Holiness, Supreme Guru, master therapist," I lay on the sofa and I put my feet on his knees. "Do you want me to talk about my daddy issues?"

Jay rolls his eyes in the most theatrical way he can manage, "Guinn, I'm being serious."

"Very well, if you don't care about my daddy issues maybe you have questions about my periods? Or my sex life?"

"I don't have any question about your sex life: the walls are pretty thin."

"That was a good one," I acknowledge without even smiling.

I don't want to talk about that night, but at the same time a knot in my chest tells me that I need to. Maybe another beer can help.

"Nope, no more than three in a row," he catches the bag with the beers before I can reach it. I almost fall off the sofa, as alcohol starts to play its games with my body. It's like drugs for my neurons.

I just stare at him.

"It was an accident, Guinn, you have to accept this."

"So I just keep going, like everything is fine and the guy is not dead?"

"I didn't say that," he scratches his ear, as he does every time he's thinking about something complicated, and he has to build the line of thoughts in his mind before he can spit it out. "You have to take whatever learning you can from what happened, and just throw away the rest."

"You make it sound easy, but how do I un-see the guy's head cracking open in my hand? How do I un-hear the paramedics declare his death?"

"We can't undo what has been done, but we can give it a purpose."

I squint at him.

"Now you know you have to work harder to manage your physical strength and control your anger," he doesn't want to lose the thoughts he has now perfectly structured in his brain. "We didn't know anger was a problem; maybe your powers increased it and you hadn't noticed, yet, but now at least we know."

Anger.

"You have to learn to fight your rage."

Rage.

"You have to learn to think harder about every move you make, every action."

"And now what? I just go to sleep and I wake up tomorrow morning as if everything was normal? I just convince myself that I can avoid thinking about it, and somehow it magically happens?"

"It will take time," he sighs and nods. "It will take sacrifice. You will have to save yourself before you can go save other people."

"Tell me about it, I haven't saved anyone in three weeks. I haven't even worn my W suit in three weeks, who can I save?"

A pale light turns on in his eyes, "So, that's what's wrong."

I don't understand.

"I thought you were down because you were reminded of the accident with the junkie, but you're not. You miss W."

I look at him and fear grabs my throat. I take my head in my hands and I weep, telling myself it's the alcohol. But it's not.

Jay pats my shoulder, caught by surprise, as I never cry. Never.

"Being W gives a meaning to the fact that my life has been completely fucked up by these powers," I sniffle and I elaborate. "Without W I'm nothing."

The words come out before I realize it, and they hit me like a punch in the face: without W I'm nothing. I guess I've known this for some time, but it's the first time I say it out loud, for my ears to hear it and my brain to record it.

"I need W," I keep going, and the thought is even more devastating than I imagined.

Jay pats my leg, "W is part of you now, as your powers are part of you. You need to accept this."

The worst side of all this is that not only my powers changed my life, but they also changed who I am at the core of my being. I'm not Guinn anymore, there's no Guinn anymore, as I now need W to feel as a whole. My body is ripped in two parts, a cheap version of Two-Face, half skinny girl and half armored hero. Which part will win over the other? There's really no competition.

"W has to come back," I announce to Jay, who's been silently observing my inner turmoil from the outside, a quiet grin deforming his regular features.

"I can't be just Guinn."

He nods.

"I'll go back to saving the world," I shout as I try to stand up from the couch, but a wave of nausea and migraine kicks me back down.

Jay grabs me by an arm before I crash on the coffee table, "Maybe not tonight," he very wisely points out.

"Maybe not tonight," I agree.

I look at him and I can swear I see him floating above the sofa, a god-like weightless being. Then I pass out.

I open my eyes. Somehow I didn't expect to wake up this time, but somehow I did. I'm still hungover from yesterday night's therapy session with Jay, and I know what I need to feel better: a yoga session with Shaila.

I check her schedule on my phone, and it's clearly my lucky day, as she teaches a 7 am class on Thursdays at the gym. Bingo.

Shaila opens her eyes wide as I walk in her yoga studio, her lips forming a clear "what the fuck". I laugh.

"New day, new Guinn," I tell her while I'm placing my mat just in front of hers.

Her voice guides me through the class for forty-five minutes, emptying my mind from all worries. I close my eyes as often as I can, to prevent from being distracted by the other attendees, an interesting mix of ages and colors, a celebration of East Harlem and its people.

"Can I offer you a cappuccino?" I ask Shaila at the end of the class.

"Don't you want to shower, first?" she jokingly smells me.

"Nah, I can go to the office like this: you know my boss likes me exactly as I am."

We both laugh and we hug each other, exploding in a joint "eew" when our grossly sticky skins touch. We look at each other and we laugh again.

"I missed you," she caresses my face. "I haven't seen you in a few weeks."

"I know."

"My next class is in two hours," she tells me with a smile as we walk towards the dressing room.

We jump in two neighboring showers, and we keep chatting about our jobs, her husband, and my messy love life.

She glimpses the gym manager right as we're walking out of the main door, and she lightly touches my shoulder, "Give me a second: I need to fix next week's schedule."

I'm waiting for her outside the gym, my nose deep in my phone, when someone brushes my back. My senses are fully alert and my muscles contract before I can even turn around to see who that might be.

"Look who's here," Matt greets me with a kiss. Right, he works at the gym in between shifts at the research center. He's even hunkier under the sun than at night.

I smile at him as he holds me in his arms.

"Are we still on for Saturday?" he seems to remember.

"The office party?"

"Yes. I hope you won't feel awkward about it: everyone is going to be there."

"All your peers, you said?" I investigate. Is there more?

"It turns out the big bosses are going to be there too. Someone apparently invited them and they all said they will show up," he nods with excitement.

A shiver rolls down my spine.

"The big bosses are coming to the party?"

"I know, totally unexpected! Doctor Bellver is surely going to be there, and even Professor Hoffmann said he might come."

I can hear blood roaring in my ears, adrenaline making my muscles contract even more. My right fist clenches, adding a new small crack to the phone it is still holding. Bellver. And Hoffmann. Both in the same place, at the same time. This is my chance to dig deeper, and maybe finally find something.

I keep my smile up and I let my breaths cool down before I enthusiastically confirm with Matt, "Let me know when and where you need me to be."

You bet I'm coming.

"Look at you two, guys," Shaila interrupts the raging flow of my thoughts. "Matt, do you want to join us for breakfast?"

"Thank you, Shaila, but I actually have a session in a few minutes. Surely next time, though: I still have to thank you for your wonderful match-making efforts," he winks.

Sweet Matt.

He kisses me and he slides in the gym's entrance.

Shaila grabs my arm and she walks me to the closest café, where we get coffees and we keep discussing things I immediately forget. My mind is focused on one topic: Saturday's party.

On the 6 train to the office I sit down and I let my head touch the wall behind me, abandoning my body to the rhythmic oscillations of the train. I close my eyes.

In my dream I'm dead. In my dreams I'm always dead.

WHEREVER
WHENEVER
10
Annalisa Conti

162

WHEREVER WHENEVER

I watch my city from up top, sitting on the edge of the Williamsburg Bridge. My spine vibrates when the M train crosses the bridge, with its late night cargo of shift workers, youngsters, and drunks. This is the best view of downtown Manhattan: the abandoned projects on Grand Street and the crime-infested Chinatown soon make room for the Manhattan Bridge and Brooklyn Bridge, South Street Seaport and Wall Street. I can't see Lady Liberty from here, but she's right behind the stump that was supposed to become the Freedom Tower, if only the city hadn't lost all its money in the wildly unsuccessful fight against crime, forcing contractors to bail out on their unpaid construction sites. The city that used to be a forest of cranes is now a haunted cemetery of interrupted buildings and empty condos. Lady Liberty's flame barely heats up anybody's heart, nowadays.

It feels good to be back in action. I forced myself to stay put for a few weeks, convinced that was the only solution to leave behind paparazzi, scrambling to get pictures and videos of me, and the Police, trying to arrest me. Chief Logan is really pissed off at me, but I don't agree with him: I don't think my presence in the city is making him look like an incompetent asshole, as I'm mostly helping him and his guys during my nighttime missions. But I don't want to stop and make conversation: I hear New York City's correctional facilities are among the worst in the country.

It's a good night to fight for justice, the air is fresh and Jay, my brilliant friend, has perfected my armor's cooling system. I stand up, hiding behind a pillar to prevent the passengers of a J train from seeing me. I stretch my arms in my black full-body suit, strategically reinforced in the right places to make me appear even bulkier, stronger. I contract and relax my face's muscles behind my mask, to release tension and find my focus in a yoga trick I learned from Shaila, my second brilliant friend.

I'm ready.

I run west on the bridge's edge, jumping over rods and around pillars. I keep hiding in the bridge's shadows, until I'm close enough to the first blocks of the Lower East Side to jump on the first roof, and disappear from any eye that could be peeking at me from the street. I venture further towards the housing blocks, and I hear the first screams. I slide down the wall of a run-down townhouse, hanging from the fire escape and looking around.

I finally see them: two guys are robbing a deli. I grin. I hate them already, small local criminals brutalizing the poor people in their own neighborhoods. It makes my adrenaline flow faster in my bloodstream, reaching every molecule of my body and making it explode with power. I know I'm not invincible, but so far I've been stabbed and shot at, and I'm still here to breathe down everybody's neck.

"Nighttime shopping?" I yell from the deli's entrance.

My voice is a thunder. I can never thank Jay enough for his best gadget, a voice modulator that he has calibrated at exactly the right frequencies, to induce fear and disorientation in those who listen. The two robbers look at me with pure terror in their eyes: they know me. They've seen my pictures in the newspapers and on everybody's Facebook, they've seen the videos of me the whole city can't shut up about. A proper smile forms on my face, too bad they can't see it.

The scene is frozen: I'm standing at the entrance, in all my towering strength; the two guys are holding the cashier, a teenager or so, by his collar, pointing a knife at his neck; the boy is yet unsure about how to express his mix of excitement and fright, so he just squeals. I sigh.

"Guys," I try to wake up everyone, shaking my head, "Let's be serious here. You, asshole number one, let the boy go."

The robbers look at each other, but they don't move. I sigh again. It's getting boring.

"Guys, focus! Do you want me to come there and do it myself?"

Yeah, that's what I thought.

I jump at them before they can react. With a punch I remove the knife from the kid's throat, and with a second punch I make sure asshole number one goes to sleep right away. Surprisingly, asshole number two attacks me with his knife, which startles me a little. But just a little. I stop him with a kick, and I break his arm with a second kick. Oh I do apologize, but sometimes I still mismanage my inhuman strength.

"Sorry bro," I pat asshole number two on the head, as he screams like a pig, holding the shattered arm with his other hand.

"Are we good here?" I ask the robbers, before turning towards the cashier, "Call the police, and tell them you have a present for them."

"You're the superhero," the boy nods.

"It's cool to be famous," I bow. "And for your reference, and for anyone on your Facebook and Instagram, I do have a name. My name is W."

God I missed W.

I get home right before dawn on a beautiful Saturday morning, and I have enough juice left in my brain to set my alarm: Matt's office summer party is later today, so I can't oversleep.

"Guinn!"

What the…

"Guinn, wake up! Your alarm has been screaming for five minutes, don't you hear it?" Jay's eyes are about to come out of their orbits.

"Relax," I squeeze his shoulder, "Did I disturb you? What were you doing that was so important?"

He sighs, "I'm skyping with grandma, ok?"

"Can I say hi to her? Please?"

Jay thinks I'm joking and he leaves my room, to go back to his bedroom and his thick family conversations, but I actually love his grandma. I blow him a kiss from my bed, and I finally stand up and I drag my feet towards the shower.

"125!" Matt texts me when he gets off the 6 subway train at 125th street, and he runs towards me at the bus stop nearby.

It's a glorious day for a party at the New York Botanical Garden, and even the bus ride from East Harlem to the Bronx is not as daunting as usual. The blinding sunlight covers up for us the habitual bus crowd of Saturday morning losers and junkies, the ghetto of Mott Haven, the flourishing drug dealing business of West Bronx, and the burned down and now abandoned buildings of what once was Fordham University. Matt holds my hand tighter and tighter during our journey through hell, and he stands right next to me to shield my body, fairly exposed in a short sleeveless dress, from wondering eyes. I do my best not to grin at his protective instinct. So cute.

As we cross the entrance of the Garden and we look for the Hudson Garden Grill, where the research facility's management planned the summer party, Matt sighs with relief. I sigh, too, but to collect my strength and prepare for whatever this day will bring me.

"Is everything fine?" Matt looks at me. His hand is on my shoulder, and he must have felt my back contracting and tensing at the idea of confronting Bellver.

I take a deeper breath to relax my muscles and I smile at him, "Sure, I'm excited!"

He kisses me on the cheek and we enter the restaurant. The waiter walks us to the outside area where cocktails are being served. Behind the trees I can see the glass walls and multicolored flowers of the Conservatory in a blur; my eyes struggle to focus on the scene in front of me, where sun umbrellas project light shades on the ground, protecting the party crowd from the unforgiving midday sun heat. I shake my head to clear my vision and my eyes scan faces to identify Bellver or Hoffman, unsuccessfully. I memorize all data in my brain, though, like a supercomputer with the sole purpose of storing information to then download to Jay. To discover my past. My mind is working faster than it ever has, processing sounds and colors, lights and smells, Matt's arm's skin I'm brushing with my fingers, the air entering my nose and rushing to my lungs, my bloodstream transporting oxygen and energy all the way to my neurons. Everything slows down and I can capture every microscopic movement: the earring swinging with the breeze on that woman's ear, the phone vibrating in that man's pocket, wine sloshing in glasses on waiters' trays. People recognize Matt and they walk towards us to greet us, so slowly that I can follow the contractions of each muscle on each face, as smiles bloom on mouths, the dance of glasses being passed from one hand to the other to shake hands with Matt, the movements and dilations of pupils focusing on me. I have never felt this powerful.

"Nice to meet you, Guinn," a man says as I shake his hand. A gust of wind on my face tells me everything got back to normal and my senses are now running at regular speed again.

I smile, "Nice to meet you, too."

We all grab wine glasses when a waiter approaches us with his tray full of reds and whites. I sip my glass of Cabernet as slowly as I can, to prevent the devastating effects of alcohol from taking control of my body. Somehow my superpowers can super-deal with anything, except a couple of drinks. Matt and his colleagues talk about work and sports and politics and life, and I ingurgitate it all.

I have barely the chance to register that it's almost time to sit down for lunch, and there is still no sign of Bellver, when Matt whispers in my ear, eyeing behind my back, "There she is, Doctor Bellver."

All my senses wake up again screaming, all alarms yelling in my mind. My fists are ready for a fight and my back contracts again, prepared to attack. I can see the woman walking towards us, an undecipherable smile on her face. Does she recognize me? I sink my eyes into hers, those eyes I so vividly remember from that night many years ago, the night of the accident, when something changed me and threw my life in the toilet for good. I keep my smile up not to let go of any of the awkwardness in front of Matt, but inside me I'm fighting a war with my own self, ripped apart by the need to restrain myself and the deep desire to claw at her neck and yell at her, "What have you done to me? Why me?"

"This is Doctor Bellver," she's now in front of me as Matt introduces us. "Doctor Bellver, this is my friend Guinn."

She nods and we prepare to shake hands. I blink. Our skins touch.

As I reopen my eyes I know I'm not in the present, nor in the Botanical Garden's restaurant, rather in a memory from the past. All is dark.

A light turns on above me, a street lamp. I'm by myself. I look around and my brain fills with knowledge: it's that night again, nine years ago. My friend Stella, whom I spent the night with from dinner to cocktails and bars, just left me to go back home to her apartment in the neighborhood, and I'm walking to the subway by myself. I'm somewhere in the Lower East Side of Manhattan. The street is gloomily empty. More street lights turn on in front of me, as to show me the way I need to follow in this memory, the same steps I took that night. I walk from street light to street light, turning left and right in the semi-darkness. I see shadows of human beings just outside the cones of light projected by the lampposts, out of reach from the corners of my memory. I hear noises of cars and people in the busy night, but it's all a background whisper, echoes from the darkness. I cross streets with no names in between buildings I can't see clearly, so I have no points of reference. I am lost, but at the same time I know where I'm going and what's about to happen. I step into the last street light's bright cone, and everything else gets back to full obscurity, all other lights are now turned off. Slowly, the bright cone expands, and second after second my understanding of where I am expands with it. I see it next to me: the research center. It appears different from today, with smaller windows and a more ancient townhouse-y look to it, as if it was simply converted from residence to lab at some point, without any further update to its external structure. This confirms for me not only where I am, but also when.

All of a sudden, a heat wave touches my skin and it burns my nose, cutting my breath. I shield my face with my arms and I take a couple of steps away from the research center, just in time to be out of reach when the building blows up in an explosion of fire and dust. The acid smell of chemicals fills the atmosphere, and I know I am breathing into them. Something in the air I am inhaling through my nose and mouth, open in a silent scream, crawls down my throat and in my lungs, in my blood, to each one of my cells, and I can feel it. Fire burns inside me. Time stops. The awareness of something horrific happening to my body makes me lose my balance and fall flat on my back on the sidewalk. I lay down for some long minutes, my eyes closed. Clouds of deadly fire vapors envelop me, leaving only darkness around me. I feel hands touching my skin, is someone here with me? I sense fingers poking me, is someone examining me? My body doesn't follow my commands and I'm not able to reopen my eyes. Who is here with me? Or is it just the hot pressure of the explosion's shockwaves on my muscles? Is my brain messing with my physical perceptions?

When I can, I channel my remaining energies on the effort of standing up again, fighting nausea and disorientation. I stumble back towards the research center, unsure of where to go or what to do now. As in a dream inside a dream, I pause and I watch firefighters braving the flames. Some of them stand in front of the building and they manoeuver a hose from the street, while a second unit is already up the ladder with a second hose to put the flames out from what remains of the roof. The building is consuming fast, and I am hypnotized by the unstoppable collapse of its structure. A third unit runs in and out the main entrance, looking for people trapped inside, but there doesn't seem to be anyone around, anyone from the lab itself. Was it empty that night? Then what the hell happened, what did ignite the explosive reaction?

From my vantage point on the left of the fire truck, I can see someone sneaking from around the corner and approaching the right side of the truck. I can't see the person's features yet, but I already know who that is. Her eyes reflect the brightness of the flames, which are still engulfing the research center, as shadows dance on her skin, deforming her face into a grotesque mask of fear and despair. She turns her head around, to check if anyone else is in the vicinity, until her eyes fall on me. I can see panic in her gaze, I can see questions overcrowding her lips. Most of all, I can see recognition: this isn't the first time she lays her eyes on me. Was she really here a few minutes ago, doing something to me, watching the effects of her wicked chemicals propagate in my body and destroy my life forever? Or was it another dream?

I blink.

"Nice to meet you, Guinn," Doctor Bellver is saying as she shakes my hand.

"Nice to meet you, ma'am," I automatically respond, fighting the shivers that slide up from my hand, still in contact with hers, and spread across my whole being.

I twist my eyes left and right to check if anybody noticed me dreaming in daylight for several minutes, before realizing it was probably all gone in just a second. Doctor Bellver lets go of my hand, and I drop back into here and now, the heat from the day and the noises and perfumes from the flowers and the party assailing me and plunging me back into reality.

"Let's sit with the guys," Matt gently pulls me out of my reveries.

I grab his hand and I follow him inside the Hudson Garden Grill, where we share a table with some of his colleagues. A tenth of my mind is enough to keep me awake and focus on lunch, to signal to me when to laugh at someone's joke, when to speak to answer questions on my personal life or my job, when to put my brain in listening mode when someone else is telling a story. The rest of me is stuck nine years ago, queries without an answer rolling on the screen in a never ending loop of question marks, unconnected pictures struggling to build a coherent movie.

It's late afternoon when I finally leave the party with Matt. I haven't talked to Doctor Bellver after our first encounter, and it is probably for the best: a mounting rage has possessed me since that first handshake. I know she was there on that day, and I am sure she concretely has responsibilities in what happened to me. I just have to find a way to remember more, to fish in my memories for more details about that night. I sigh.

"I hope you didn't get too bored," Matt kisses me on the cheek while we wait for the bus to bring us back to 125th street in East Harlem.

"It was very educational," I reassure him.

Even more than you think, Matt.

"Do you want to stop at your place for a little while?" he offers. I stare at him. "Or we can go to my place, even if it's further downtown. Whatever you prefer."

I normally would jump on the concrete opportunity of a high quality shag, but right now my mind is wandering too far away in time and space.

I scramble for excuses, checking the time on my phone, "It's quite late, and I still have a couple of errands to run…"

He smiles, his macho-with-a-heart wide-teethed grin, "No worries, I am fairly wiped out by this full day with my colleagues, and I can understand if you're fed up with me for this weekend. Too bad Professor Hoffman didn't make it, as I would have loved you to meet him, as well."

I had completely forgotten about the Professor, focused as I am on Doctor Bellver and her own role in the events. But Matt is unknowingly right to bring the Professor up again: what's his own role in the story? Was he there? Is he aware of whatever Doctor Bellver did to me that night? More questions, and still no answers.

"I'm definitely not fed up with you," I kiss him on the lips, grabbing his ass to highlight the concept.

He laughs out loud as we part ways at the 6 subway stop, where he takes a train downtown and I slowly walk home.

Images from my daydream linger before my eyes as I pace South in East Harlem, and they accompany me home where I find Jay, busy with the latest episode of something.

"Did you meet Doctor Bellver?" he asks me as soon as I open the door.

I sigh in response.

"And?"

"I had another vision," I respond, before dragging him in my black hole of memories through the flames.

He shakes his head in the end, "We still are not sure if she was there that night…"

"What?" I can't contain myself, "I told you she was there. I saw her!"

"You said it yourself: you're not sure if someone was there with you right after the explosion of if you were just dazed and imagined things."

He is right, he is always right.

"What do I do now?"

"You need to remember more details from that night," Jay thinks out loud.

"You make it sound easy, buddy, but it took me nine years to find just this one small thing."

"I know," he rubs my shoulder. "Let me think through it."

"And what do I do in the meantime, while you meditate, you look for the perfect solution to all our problems, and maybe you also fix world hunger and wars in the meantime?"

He grins, "You're smart, Guinn, look for evidence, look for clues. Use Matt to find information and potentially to build other opportunities to meet with Doctor Bellver. I don't know, do they have a Christmas office party?"

"Christmas is months from now, Jay."

"So what? You're young, you have all the time in the world," he shrugs.

"Right, if a criminal organization doesn't kill me in the meantime. Or the Police don't shoot me. Or I don't drown in the East River trying to jump from a bridge. Remember, I'm awesome but not immortal."

"Well, what do you want me to tell you?" he opens his arms. "Go out, don't get murdered, and enjoy being a superhero!"

178

ACKNOWLEDGMENTS

The first thanks always go to Emmanuel, who so selflessly supports me, and who still believes in me after all these years.

Most readers wouldn't have this book in their hands if it weren't for Lore, who is my publicist and my agent, my finger on the pulse and my friend. Many readers wouldn't have noticed this book on a shelf or in an online list if it weren't for Valeria's outstanding cover art and design, and her ongoing work to bring to life my thoughts and feelings about Guinn and W. I owe both of you guys way more than the credit your work deserves. Let's keep redefining modern feminism and #superheroes together!

ABOUT THE AUTHOR

Annalisa Conti lives and writes in New York City, where she has been spending the last few years of her life. She is a woman who writes about women, real human beings facing drama and challenges, finding happiness and rewards, succeeding and failing. Normal people.

If you like Jane Austen for her honest humor, Gillian Flynn for her descent into human darkness, and Elena Ferrante for her focus on storytelling, you will find Annalisa's tales wildly entertaining.

She recently published her third novel, NINE. It is a modern tale on motherhood, a unique story about pregnancy, its hidden fears, and its untold truths.

Her second novel, AFRICA, was an Amazon Kindle #1 in its category. Reviewers say it is a "fascinating" "astonishing" story of a life-changing journey to the end of the world, "powerful and dramatic, and well integrated into this incredible "decorum"".

Annalisa is also the author of ALL THE PEOPLE, a novel built around a woman's secrets. Reviewers say "you cannot put it down", it is "capturing reader's attention since the very first lines", and it has a "very deep and accurate psychological perspective".

She publishes quarterly episodes in the collection of short stories THE W SERIES, which describe the world of W, a superhero like no other. Reviewers say it is "a classic action story but somehow very different from anything else", with a "writing style packed of action and visual clues as if it was taken right out of a Marvel comic strip".

The first ten episodes of THE W SERIES have been collected in W IS FOR WONDER.

Find more at:
www.annalisaconti.com
Twitter @AnnalisaContiUS
www.facebook.com/AnnalisaContiAuthor

BOOKS BY THIS AUTHOR

Please visit your favorite book and ebook retailers to discover books by Annalisa Conti:

Nine, a novel (2018)
Africa, a novel (2015)
All The People, a novel (2014)

W Is For Wonder, a collection of short stories (2018)

The W Series, short stories (from 2016)